Also by Scott Geisel

JACKSON FLINT MYSTERIES
Fair Game
Water to Bind

OTHER NOVELS
Miller Knew: An Appalachian Noir and Suspense Story

JACKSON FLINT SHORTS
Masquerade
Escape Velocity

OTHER SHORTS
Cinderbox Road & Other Stories

WHEAT PENNY

A Jackson Flint mystery
Yellow Springs, Ohio

Scott Geisel

Jackson Flint
Detective Agency
Yellow Springs, Ohio

#YellowSpringsMysteries

Fox&
Possum
PUBLISHING

scottgeisel.com

Printed and published in the United States of America.

First edition: February 2, 2024

Cover art and book design copyright © 2024 by Pam Geisel.

ISBN 978-1-7350183-5-5

Dedicated to Liz Valenti and Ann Simonson, and to the wonderful restaurant Wheat Penny in Dayton, Ohio

1

THE KID WAS ACTING UP. Given what he'd been through, I didn't blame him. I could even feel a little sorry for him. But there are limits.

I figured Quando for fifteen. His actual age hadn't been established. There was a lot about him that hadn't been established. That was part of the problem.

Quando had dropped into my life oddly and unexpectedly a month before in a mall parking lot. It hadn't gone well. First off, I was at a mall. Don't get me wrong. I understand the attraction for people who like that kind of thing. But put me in a quiet open space or any place that's not around a lot of people, cars, and blacktop, and I'll be a lot happier than inside an urban box where I might think buying a few things could make me happy for a minute.

So when Quando had arrived walking across the parking lot with his friend, and his friend was carrying a big stack of money and a gun, I was already itchy. Plus, it was my experience that most often guns and money don't play well together. Put teens in the mix, and things go downhill even faster. That was strike two.

The other kid with Quando wanted to show off his money and his gun. See, there's the thing—teens and guns and money. I was the only other person visible in the parking lot. That made me the target.

It wasn't a smart thing for the kid to do. When you're doing things you're not supposed to, showing off makes it harder to get away with those things. Add that I was a lot bigger than the kids, trained in self-defense and subject restraint, licensed and carrying a firearm in my vehicle, and a former county deputy, and this kid was truly making a mistake. It probably wasn't his first.

Quando's buddy came right at me and demanded that I pay homage to his stack of dirty bills. When I wasn't impressed, he thought the gun might get him more respect. That's the weird thing about people. You've got a big stack of money and a gun, but you can't just go off and be satisfied with that. You've got to bully and show off and get attention to feel good. In my line of work, I'd seen my share of that. It always made me wonder.

I was trying to dial things down and get out of there, but this kid had other things on his mind. It was getting ugly when my friend Brick, who I'd been waiting on so I could get away from the mall, swooped in and broke up the party.

Brick doesn't take any shit. What was going down got under his skin and he chased Quando and his agitated friend and whoever was lurking in a van that was circling the lot, probably the guys who were waiting for the stack of money to be delivered to them.

Brick sent me home before the chase. Normally this isn't something we would do. Your buddy shows up to help you out of a jam, you stick around until the fight is over. That's the way it works.

But Brick had taken a special interest in these kids. He wanted to make sure they got the entire message he was trying to tell them.

Part of it was, Brick and I also had some other understandings. My prime objective was to stay safe and go home every day to raise my daughter. We agreed on that.

Brick didn't have any kids. His priority was to try to manage some lingering repressed feelings about his service as an ex-Marine. When he showed up in the parking lot with the kid there waving his gun, Brick sent me home to protect my main interest. He indulged his own demons by chasing the kids down when they ran.

Later when Brick clammed up about what happened with the two kids, and nothing made the evening news and he didn't get shot up and I didn't have to bail him out of the slam, I figured that was the end of it. But then Quando turned up at Brick's cabin in the woods. There wasn't an explanation. Quando was just there. It had been more than a month now. And the kid wasn't adjusting well.

Quando wasn't in school, no one had shown up looking for him, and Brick didn't know what to do with the kid. Nothing was established. Neither of them was talking about it. That was a problem.

But for the current moment, Brick and I were doing something familiar and comfortable. We were running up the devil's backbone.

The kid skulked unhappily at the bottom of the hill.

The devil's backbone is a narrow road that twists up between the Glen Helen nature preserve and John Bryan State Park. It's scenic and shaded. It's also steep.

I run the hill to keep in shape so I can catch the bad guys in my work for my detection agency. My business cards read *Jackson Flint Detective Agency, Yellow Springs, Ohio. Professional. Discreet.* I was the only detective in the village, so I could add *discrete*. But who likes a geeky P.I.?

Truth be told, given the current culture and the funky vibe of our little village, I should think I was running up the backbone to stay in shape to catch the bad guys, bad girls, men, women, non-binaries, otherwise defined, or non-gender-defined individuals. But mostly it was bad guys.

I also liked the devil's backbone because getting to the top first was one of the few things I could regularly beat Brick at. The hill gets steeper and the turns get tighter near the top. It was oxygen-deficit territory.

Brick wasn't beating me on the hill, but you don't mess with a Marine. Once a Marine, always a Marine. They never give up.

Our legs pumped out a steady pace through the September air. Brick's dark arms glided in short, controlled arcs, biceps bulging beneath a sleeveless shirt that said *You're Not Ready for Me.* My euro-white arms flashed pale stripes against his guns.

Brick found some breath and pulled up beside me. He spoke without looking over. "Today is the day."

I lifted my knees and pulled a step ahead again. "It's not a competition."

I couldn't see it, but I knew Brick grinned. He reclaimed the step. "It never is."

"It'd be a competition if you could run faster."

He grunted and I felt him throw an elbow. I dodged, and the elbow missed. Brick fell back a step again and I heard his words fade behind me. "Jackson, what did I tell you about trying to be funny?"

"Keep working at it?"

He tried again to close the gap. "No. That's not it."

We cut through a tight turn and the road steepened. I stepped up the pace and put more space between us and called over my shoulder. "This is the hard part." I ran faster. "This is the part that always gets you."

Brick wasn't done. The Marine in him made him put his head down and push. I let him come up beside me. He was breathing hard. "Today is the day."

The last long steep stretch opened above us. I sucked air and told my legs to loosen.

Brick pretended to stumble. I looked over. When I slowed, he took off, arms and legs pumping like cogs on a steam train.

A trick. He lurched ahead.

But there's a switch in me. It doesn't like to be beat. I can't stop it. The switch just flips. It pushes me past what I think are my limits. Past reason and thinking into just *go*. It opens all the cylinders at once and burns everything until there's nothing left.

Brick knew about the switch. He was timing his run to make the top before I could kick into gear.

The switch opened. My legs lifted and my lungs expanded. Everything went blank except *run, fast, now*.

I closed the gap to Brick, our arms pumping like dueling pistons. I tasted iron and adrenaline and lost any control of moderation. The switch was wide open. I would run faster until I reached the top or passed out.

I didn't say I like the switch. It just works that way sometimes. I didn't even see Brick when I chugged by. I was just running.

When Brick found me at the top of the hill lying on the blacktop trying to gulp oxygen, my vision blurred to tones of sepia, he leaned down. "Jackson, you are a freak."

"Kind of you to say it." I rolled over onto my knees. "I know you mean that in a good way."

He folded himself over the guardrail and sucked air. "You tell yourself what you need to."

I would have grinned if I had more oxygen.

Then Brick pushed himself off the rail and started walking down the hill. "That's one."

I knew his game. We planned to run eight hills. When I had spent everything on that, he'd make it ten. If he hadn't beaten me by ten, he'd say let's do twelve. Eventually I had to fall down.

I walked down next to Brick and pretended I wasn't breathing heavy. "I could do this all day."

He said nothing. We kept walking.

Quando came into view below, noodling around at the edge of the road near the trees.

"How're things going with the kid?"

Brick grunted. "Could be better. He grumbles a lot."

That was putting it mildly. The kid sulked. When he did talk, it was usually to complain about something.

"Think he'll run today?"

Brick grunted again. "Said he would. But look."

I gave the next thing a second of thought before I let it out. "He in school?"

Brick raised an eyebrow and dropped it.

That meant no. Quando had arrived at Brick's cabin at the beginning of the school year. There hadn't been any contact with Quando's family or parents, and nothing about the bangers he'd been with when we found him. Nothing about the big stack of money they'd been carrying. Quando was a blank slate, or pretended to be.

I figured that was all we were going to talk about it, but Brick said, "Kid doesn't seem to be happy."

I didn't guess so.

"He wanted to come. Now he doesn't want to run."

I knew why. "Won't run because he doesn't like to lose."

Brick dropped his head. "We been through that. He's not going to get stronger if he doesn't try."

"He's young. That hasn't stuck yet."

Brick sighed, a very manly sigh of the kind that only a heavily muscled ex-Marine can make. "He doesn't seem to be happy about anything."

That wasn't exactly a surprise. And that wasn't the whole of Brick's problem. This wasn't an old cowboy movie where you just picked up a kid on the trail and he became your son and you raised him into a right good man. Someone should have come looking for Quando, or asking questions.

We reached the bottom of the hill and stopped where Quando was slouched onto a large block of limestone. Brick looked down at Quando's closed hand. "You find something?"

Quando's eyes looked bored. It may have been real or an act. Either way, it was convincing.

Brick pointed. "Show me."

The bored look stayed there, but Quando opened his hand and turned his palm and extended his fingers. Olive-tinged skin caught sunlight that drifted down through the trees. He was lighter than Brick but had some color. I wondered what heritage the kid might call his own. At the rate he talked, I might never know.

Something glinted in Quando's hand. He pushed his palm closer so we could see. "It ain't nothing."

I looked. "A wheat penny."

"It was weird, so I picked it up."

"I haven't seen one of those for a long time."

"It's literally nothing."

I reached toward Quando's hand. "It's literally a penny."

Quando pulled his hand away and drew his arm back as if to throw the penny into the woods.

I held up a hand. "Wait."

Quando's arm stopped. "It ain't worth nothing."

"People used to save these."

"For what? What they could buy with them?"

"No, just because…it's different."

"How is that worth anything?"

I frowned. Did he really want me to explain it, or was this just part of the teen ethos? "Don't things just sometimes make you happy? Just because of what they are?"

Quando looked at the penny in his hand. "Like what?"

"What do you mean, like what?"

"Like what would make you happy?"

"Like anything. Like—a sunset."

"A sunset?"

"You know, when the sun appears to drop below the horizon because of the rotation of the earth." I regretted my choice of words. His snark was contagious.

"How does a sunset make you happy?"

"It's pleasant. It's simple. It's nice to look at. It's relaxing."

"That literally happens everyday. It ain't nothing. I repeat: how can a sunset make you happy?"

And here was that loop the kid could draw you into. I shrugged. "It doesn't have to take a lot. Just what's there in front of you."

"Like this penny?"

"Yeah, like that penny."

"It makes you happy?"

"Yeah, it makes me happy."

"So you want it?"

"Sure, if you don't."

Then Quando drew his arm back again as if to throw the penny into the trees.

I turned away. Damn, the kid could be unpleasant.

And he wasn't done. "You know what'd make me happy?"

I didn't answer.

Quando held his hands out ten inches apart. "A big stack of money. Twenty thousand dollars."

There it was. One of the conversations no one had been having. One of the things that was left unsettled. Quando hadn't gotten his share of the stack of money.

I stepped away. This was something I didn't want to be in the middle of.

Quando followed me and showed me he still had the coin in his hand. "That's twenty thousand times more happiness than this penny."

I wasn't going to say anything. I truly tried to stop myself. But it had to come out. "Do the math."

"Huh?"

"Twenty thousand dollars is two million times more than a penny."

"Two hundred, two million, what's the difference?"

I frowned. "That's what we were talking about."

He didn't get it.

I should have stopped. But the dam had been breached. "Look, you weren't going to get the whole thing anyway. You were delivering that stack of money to someone else. You were only going to get a cut."

Quando's agitated look told me he didn't like what I was saying.

"So you were going to get what? Maybe a thousand?"

He stared.

"So say a thousand. A hundred thousand times the value of that penny. What would you do with a hundred thousand times that penny? Would that give you a hundred thousand times more satisfaction?"

He snorted like I was stupid. Maybe so.

"I'm just saying, if that penny can bring a little satisfaction for someone, why not just let there be some happiness for a moment?"

Quando held his hands out in mock surrender. "This is stupid." He walked away.

I started jogging back up the hill.

Brick came beside me.

I picked up the pace. "Sorry."

"For what?"

"I just made things worse."

Brick looked over his shoulder down at Quando. "I doubt it." Then he reconsidered. "But you didn't help much."

"You think?"

We cruised through a turn. Brick was not going to beat me today.

He said, "And you're so good with your daughter."

"It doesn't seem to translate." It was easier with Cali. She was a good kid. She always had been. Sure, she was a teenager and her brain was racing with hormones and incomplete connections in the frontal lobe where decisions were processed. But all teenagers faced that. Even when

Cali and I had endured the loss of her mother and my wife, she had kept a good and stable head on her when others might have struggled more. Maybe a lot more.

I rolled my neck to loosen some muscles. "Cali's a good kid."

Brick was already breathing harder to keep up. "Maybe Quando can be too."

I guess that was it in a nutshell. How do you get from here to there when you don't know the way and there is no roadmap? "I don't suppose you could do some of that drill sergeant stuff with him, could you?"

Brick's face flashed a frown.

"You know, an ex-Marine like you. Put a little discipline into the kid."

"This isn't the military. There's a fine line here. Or a big muddy line. I've pushed him. But Quando is young and he's had a tough road. He's what we would call untrainable. They send those boys home. They flush out."

I nodded. But I didn't know. I hadn't been in the military. Police training doesn't count.

Brick knew. "Quando has already flushed out. Why he's with me now. He needs something more than just discipline."

The words were on the tip of my tongue. He needs a home. He needs to go to school. You can't just keep him. He's not a puppy. But I kept all of those thoughts in.

The top of the hill came into sight and teased us.

Brick stayed with me. "I'm in no position to…the kid just…came home with me. I didn't think about what would come next."

It was the last steep stretch. The switch was calling. I resisted and stayed back with Brick.

"I ain't exactly a father figure. I know we can't keep on like this, but I don't know what comes next." It was the most Brick had talked about the kid. "I can't just turn him back out on the street. And I can't—"

Then Brick tried to gain the hill. Maybe another trick. It didn't matter. I took the top before him again.

We walked back down quietly until Brick said, "You make it look easy with Cali."

"A lot of things are different with her. Pretty much everything with Cali is different than with Quando."

He nodded.

"And there've been some bumps with Cali." He didn't ask, but I thought he wanted to know. "Cali doesn't like that Marzi and I are taking things slow. She wants Marzi around more. It's getting a little… testy."

Marzi and I had started dating during the summer. Cali had been really excited about it. That surprised me. I thought she'd be slow to accept anyone after losing her mother.

Brick raised an eyebrow.

"Yeah, so Marzi and I have slowed things down a bit."

The eyebrow stayed raised.

"Marzi doesn't like my line of work. Thinks it's too dangerous."

The eyebrow went down. He got it. "That makes this thing I want to ask you a little trickier."

Hmm.

"So I was hoping I could talk to Marzi."

I waited. But that was it. "Uh-huh." That was Jackson-speak for tell me more.

"And I want to know if it's OK with you."

"If what's OK?"

"If I talk to Marzi."

I looked at him. "What?"

"I want to know if I can talk to Marzi."

I stopped walking.

Brick was caught off guard and walked back to me.

"Of course you can talk to Marzi. Why do you have to ask me? What do you want to talk to her about?"

"About Quando."

"Uh-huh." Tell me more.

"I need to know if I have any—options."

"Options?"

"I mean like legally. And if I don't, what happens to the kid."

"I thought you called Samuel Thomas about that." The lawyer with two first names. He'd been involved in a case I took in the early summer. Good guy for a lawyer.

"I didn't call him."

Now I raised an eyebrow, except my eyebrows aren't as refined as Brick's, and both eyebrows went up.

"I want to talk to Marzi first."

"So talk to her."

We descended the hill.

"Why'd you think you should ask me about talking with Marzi?"

"Just did."

And that was it. We reached the bottom and ran up the devil's backbone again. And again, and several more times.

Today was not the day for Brick to beat me.

We chit-chatted as we walked down between runs. No more heavy stuff. Brick was still working on restoring a 1966 Shelby GT-350. He described that and some references to a vague kind of contract work that sounded like he couldn't tell me what he was really doing. I never knew exactly what he did to pay the bills. Maybe he used what he got from his time in the service.

I told him I had a case doing a security check for a local company that built secret things for the government. He got interested. "Physical or cyber?"

"Physical or cyber what? The things they make?"

"No, physical or cyber security check?"

"Oh. Both."

"You'll want J'Leah for the cyber."

"I'll want her for both. I couldn't do the cyber without her."

We were nearing the bottom of the hill again. We'd run up nine times. Quando had wandered off long ago, his nose in his phone and buds in his ears.

Brick walked straight past the bottom of the hill to where the Shelby was parked. I followed to my old Silverado and pulled out my phone and a water bottle.

Quando sat in the Shelby with the top down, looking at his phone. Brick came over. I reached through the truck window and set the phone on the dash. "I have to go. New client."

"You said."

"The situation is a little unusual."

Brick's gaze slid from me to Quando. "Yeah."

I climbed into the truck and gave a little finger-point to Quando. Just trying to lighten the mood. Say I was sorry without saying it. Like guys do.

Quando grinned at me and held his hand up. The penny was resting in his palm.

I smiled. He hadn't thrown it.

Then Quando cocked his arm and whipped his hand forward to throw the penny into the woods.

Like I said, you feel a little sorry for the kid, but there are limits. I drove away without looking back.

2

CLIENTS CAN BE TRICKY. There are some lines I don't like to cross. Divorce, adultery, revenge. That kind of work paid well, and there was plenty of it. Men, women, lawyers, friends, mothers-in-law, you name it. No one seemed immune from that kind of business, or the aching desperation that often came with it.

Also: no lies. A client who won't tell me what they really want isn't worth the headache and trouble that will come with the case.

And I don't work for assholes. That one explains itself.

And the most important rule: my daughter stays safe. This one is tougher. There are a lot of crazies out there, and with all of the digital eyes and ears and the internet and endless connectivity it's hard to keep your private life private. There was a time when if you could spot a tail, you had a decent chance of your work not following you home in this line of business. Now if someone had a beef or got paroled or didn't like a P.I. nosing into their business, it might bring them to my doorstep, or my daughter. This one kept me up some nights. Literally.

And a corollary: I stay safe for Cali. She's already lost her mother. My number one job every day is to come home to her. I don't carry a gun unless I think I'll need one. And if I think I might need one, I'd better think hard about how I'm going to get through that day.

I was trained as a deputy for the county sheriff. Leaving the gun at home goes against the rules. It also goes against Brick's advice. Working special ops for the military brands a special kind of caution into your psyche. Brick tried to distill that into me. He was still working on it. We've had more than one debate about whether carrying the gun kept me safer or brought more chance for trouble. I was often undecided.

A lot of the rules came down to finding the right clients, with the right cases. A good client is like a cool breeze on a hot summer day. They don't come by all that often, and they pass all too quickly. And they leave you guessing when another is going to come along.

I had high hopes for this new guy. Carlos DeLuna had come to me by referral, and I liked the person who had referred him.

We were set to meet at Carlos' office in a strip of buildings tucked beside the road between the state university and the Air Force base in Fairborn. A lot of military contractors camped out in that prime area where they could get government money from the base and research grants from the school.

It was a twenty-minute drive. On the way, Neil Young came on the radio and sang to me how sweet life would be if he could find his cinnamon girl. I'd found my cinnamon girl and married her, and life was as sweet as Neil crooned. But I'd lost my girl, and now things weren't as sweet.

I switched the dial and found Linda Ronstadt. I let it play. You always let Linda play.

Building security was light, and DeLuna had put my name on the call sheet. I walked right in. When I'd made my way up to DeLuna's office on the third floor of his building, his door was open. I went in and held my hand out across his desk.

Carlos stood, took my hand, and closed his other over the top of our shake. His grip was firm. If he were running for office, that might make me want to vote for him.

"Mister Flint. I'm happy to meet you."

"Jackson."

We released our hands and I sat. Carlos pulled his chair around from behind his desk and faced me. "I realize you'll be on the clock."

He was being generous, or figurative. There was no clock. I hadn't signed onto the case yet. We'd discussed the general parameters of the job. I was here for details. If I liked them, I would sign. And there would be no clock. The offer was a package deal. A flat rate. The money was good, real good. I was all ears.

Carlos waved a hand like he was conducting music only he could hear. "I suppose we could have completed things with a phone call and sharing some files, but I've got a bit of the old country in me."

I had detected the accent when we'd talked. Now I took in the sandy tint to Carlos' complexion, the black hair, thick mustache, and wide shoulders. I said, "You won't be offended if I guess where you're from?"

A grin slipped onto his face. The hand conducted again, a minor flourish. "Not at all."

"Mexico. Maybe Portugal. My third guess is Brazil or Argentina. I suppose that makes four guesses. You usually only get three."

The grin on his face held. "Very good. My family is long time from a very small village near San Luis Potosí. I grew up there and traveled to Mexico City to go to Universidad Nacional Autónoma de México, where I learned among other things how to speak English so well." The pride came through in every accented syllable. "And you, Mister Flint? May I guess your heritage?"

"Jackson," I repeated.

"Apologies. This formality too comes from the old country."

I nodded.

"And I may guess?"

"Please do."

He put a finger to his lips and raised his eyes in a thoughtful gesture. Then he looked me in the eye. "I think you are of European descent."

I'd expected more.

Carlos laughed at my expression. "I am sorry again. This is something of an old joke in my family. It is not meant to offend."

I laughed with him. "Ah, very good. No offense. I look like my German ancestors. There's some Swiss and Serbian mixed in."

Carlos leaned back in his seat and spread his arms in a welcoming gesture. "We laugh together. I had thought that we might get along."

"Well, you come by good referral."

"Missus Winstrop."

"Elizabeth, yes."

"I worked with her husband. Robert."

Her late husband. I'd taken a case at the beginning of the summer to search for Elizabeth's lost daughter after Robert died unexpectedly of a heart attack. "The microencapsulator."

Carlos looked surprised. "Among other ventures. Robert was an innovator of many things. And a good businessman."

He had been. Robert Winstrop's name on more than one local business attested to that.

Carlos clasped the armrest on his chair with both hands and pushed himself up. "But your time is valuable. As is mine." He went behind his desk and touched a button on a micro projector. White light sprang from the lens and framed a square on the wall where a screen descended with a mechanical whirr. Carlos touched a thin laptop computer that was open on his desk. "Let me show you some photos."

An image danced from the projector to the screen on the wall. An aerial view of a farmstead showed several buildings set back from a rural road. A narrow dirt drive tracked between fields and opened to a barn, farmhouse, and outbuildings. All of the structures had clean white paint and new green metal roofs.

Carlos zoomed in on an image. "Drone video and stills."

I nodded. I'd seen some of this before, when I requested details to consider if we should meet.

The closer view showed improvements and fortifications. The perimeter was lined by high fencing topped with coiled barbs. An entry point showed a tiny shack, electronic equipment, and an automated gate.

Carlos tapped something and the view zoomed in again to the entry gate. "There's not usually a person at the guard shack. There was when we started. But now everything has moved inside." Carlos glanced at me as if to ask if I had any questions.

I twirled my fingers for him to go on.

"Entry is automated. Visitors can be given a one-time access code that is time sensitive. Or they can be checked and admitted manually. That's when a guard would come out."

He zoomed back out to a view of the entire compound and picked up a pen from his desk. He flipped the pen around and pressed the side to activate a laser pointer in the end. "The security office is here." A red laser dot indicated the front-facing portion of the building inside the fence nearest the entry gate. The entire structure made a large rectangle.

This I already knew. The perspective and angles of the photos were different from what Carlos had sent me, but the information was essentially the same. I summoned some patience and tried to settle in. "It looks like a pole barn on steroids."

Carlos grinned. "Poured concrete slabs, steel reinforcement and doors, secure windows. But on its surface it has a beauty that flatters the original architecture of the farmstead and belies what is inside." He swept his hands in a gesture that was suggestive of a feminine form. "Like a strong woman in a fine dress."

It was a line I could never imagine using. From me it would just sound wrong. But Carlos seemed to make it work. I tilted my head. "As you say."

He pointed the dot on a modest structure at the rear of the compound. "This holds a generator and other electrical and power infrastructure." The dot moved to an exterior cinder block wall made of three sides and no roof. "The propane tank for the generator is also secure." The tank was tucked inside the walls, and fencing ran across the front.

Carlos watched for a moment as I made some quick notes in a small notepad.

Then he ran the red dot from the buildings to the old farm driveway and followed that all the way out to the country road where the property sat. "The power line is vulnerable. So that's why the generator. We have never had an interruption to continuous power on the premises."

That was something. In Ohio, especially in the rural areas, the weather could take out power during any season. Wind, storms, snow, even trees that got too close to the power lines or a squirrel that got into the wrong place or nibbled the wrong wire could take you off the grid.

The red dot flicked again. "The barn is not secure. That's just for fun, and storage. But the old farmhouse"—the laser dot settled in the center of the compound—"is a fortress. That holds the offices where most of the work gets done. The house has additions here"—the dot wiggled—"and here"—wiggling again. "And the original cellar has been expanded and reinforced. But inside…" He shrugged.

"Beautiful like a woman?" I tried.

I couldn't deliver the line like him, but Carlos accepted it. "It is charming."

I made a few more notes. "Cameras?"

"Everywhere. On the premises and also at the road." He lit the laser pointer again and picked out some points where the cameras were mounted. The dot drifted away from the compound to the front of the property.

I leaned forward.

Carlos noticed my attention.

"I didn't see those."

His eyes came up in a question.

"When I drove past. I didn't see the cameras at the road."

Carlos shut the laser light off. "You've been to the property?"

"I drove past."

"Only to drive past on the road? Not beyond?"

"That's right."

He flipped the laser pen once through his fingers.

I watched him. "Does that raise a concern for you?"

"No. It will be all right. But you will be on the recording." The pen flipped once again, forward then back. "But no matter. It is just another vehicle driving by. And no reason to notice it. The tapes are not reviewed unless there is a reason."

I considered telling Carlos that an old pickup moving slowly down a back road was about as common as you might get in Ohio, but instead I wrote a casual note on my pad.

Carlos watched me again. "And you had no trouble finding the location?"

I looked up. "The address for CDE Enterprises—your company—is listed for here, where we are sitting now. But property recorded for CDE Enterprises, LLC in Clark County also includes a rural address. That address is where the photos we're looking at were taken."

Carlos nodded. He didn't look impressed, and he didn't say *very good.* Which it wasn't. This was basic stuff. I liked to know who I was working for.

I tapped my pen on my notepad, then pointed a finger at the image on the wall. "Those fields are planted."

"They are." Carlos rotated through more images and stopped on a wider view of the property, then another. Both showed the farm compound surrounded on all sides by fields planted with a low crop cover. "Soybeans. We used to allow corn, but soy is better for keeping a line of sight open. The security people prefer it." The image switched again, this time to a combine moving through the fields and trailing a large cloud of plant dust. "The lands are leased for farming."

I tried to remember what the drive to the farmstead had been like. Typical Midwest rural routes in farm country. Some houses, lots of fields, copses of trees following the creeks and waterways between the fields. "And the neighbors? What do they think?"

"They are used to us. We are good neighbors. They don't ask questions." He pointed the dot at the image of the fields and ran the beam down to the front of the property again. "The buildings are set back substantially from the road. Trees and other growth along the front edge provide a screen. Better when the leaves are on the trees, but it is mostly private year-round."

It was a good setup. "How many employees at CDE?"

"Twenty full-time on average. Sometimes more. Sometimes less. Plus some part-time and contract work."

I wrote that down. "And how many on security?"

"Three full-time, in three shifts. Two others are part-time or rotate in as needed." He continued before I could ask the next question. "It is required for our contracts. As the business expanded and we moved into more sensitive areas of technological development, we had to either enhance security or move to a more secure location in the city."

"Like we are now?"

"Not quite. This is..." He waved a hand.

"Too easy to get in?"

The hand stopped conducting. It hadn't found the note it was seeking. "This office is good for appearances. Clients like to meet here. It is rather public."

"Why not just get a secure location on the Air Force base?"

Carlos set the pointer pen and the clicker on his desk and sat down again in the chair facing me. "You assume correctly that CDE has agreements with government and military contractors. That is where much of our revenue and grant funding comes from. Most others would have simply chosen to move to a more secure location, as you say, inside the base perimeter. That option was available to us. It has in fact been challenging to secure the work that we do at our remote location."

He sighed.

I waited.

"My brother Drummond and I, we grew up in the country. We were lucky it was out of the desert and high enough in the hills for crops to grow. We are not urban people." He sighed again. "And our work has been lucrative. We can afford to keep the rural location."

I leaned back. "The situation is unusual."

"That's why you are here." Carlos bent forward to close the distance I'd opened between us, beckoning like an old friend. "The uniqueness of the setting has raised some concerns. I thought we were past that, but now things change and we must show again that our work area is secure."

I shifted in my seat. "What things have changed, Carlos?"

His head bowed. "I must sell my half of the business."

It wasn't what I expected. I waited for more.

It didn't take long for Carlos to offer up the rest of it. "My wife. Judy. She—Judy has been a sweetheart. All these years while I've worked long hours. Squeezing in time with her around my work. She's waited. I've been promising her a second honeymoon, a long trip to all the places she's wanted to go…"

"And you want to take her now?"

Carlos' eyes had grown big and sad. "I have to take her now. Judy has—she's in remission. She may stay in remission for the rest of her life. Or she may not."

I didn't ask him what type of cancer his wife had, or the prognosis or any details. That was personal. I'd gotten the message.

"I must sell my part of the business. For the money. And for the time. I must be with Judy now."

It made sense.

"But my brother, he doesn't want me to sell."

I waited again. That usually worked.

Carlos offered up more details again. "Two things. Drum has been— he has questioned the security of our work in public ways that…have made a sale difficult."

"Why would he do that?"

"He prefers not to gain a new partner. An unknown. Someone who isn't family."

I made some notes.

"I offered to let Drum buy me out. But he can't afford it. I offered payments, time, deferred interest, no interest. He cannot do this."

"Is it the money? He can't raise financing against the collateral of the business?"

"There is another thing. Drum is the…he's not—he didn't develop the technology that…"

"He's not the brains of the operation."

Carlos tipped his head. "That's one way to say it. He didn't develop any of the proprietary information. Drum has skills. He can sell the technology. He can glad-hand and make you feel like you want to do anything to please him. He brings the contracts, the money. People feel confident in what Drum tells them."

"It seems your brother could do OK in the business without you."

"I don't know why he's worried. He would own it all. Innovation may be harder to come by, but CDE has developments that are highly desirable."

"Will you tell me again what kind of work CDE does?"

"I haven't told you once, Jackson."

I was pleased that he'd called me Jackson. And pleased that he was aware, as I was, that he hadn't disclosed the nature of the work of his company. I tried another tack. "Have you thought about simply giving your half of the business to your brother?"

Carlos raised three fingers. "There is a third thing. Drum has not been careful with his spending. There has been gambling." The fingers went down. "It is a problem." Carlos lingered over a long breath, then he looked resigned and continued. "It has threatened his clearance. This looks bad on a security check, which several of our clients have request-ed. It is a vulnerability. Drum could be leveraged because of his debts. It is a risk too for the company, but I have tried to cover for him. If I find a buyer, Drum will probably have to sell his share of CDE as well."

I made notes. "Uh-huh."

"But first we must show that the property is secure. To attract a buyer."

"You could relocate."

"That would take time, and Judy is…" He held a hand out, steady, to indicate something I didn't quite understand. "Healthy now. We must go now."

I tapped my pen. Thinking. It seemed to add up, but something felt soft about it. "You believe that the security check you have asked me to do will be sufficient for your needs? Why not do a full military check?"

His eyes came up at the word military. "I want the property checked, and the security of the information confirmed. A full military clearance check would also likely dig into my brother's personal life in a way that may create more jeopardy than advantage."

That felt right enough. I'd been interviewed for security checks on friends who worked at the base. They asked some tough questions.

Carlos stood. "And your tech person. You have someone. He comes highly recommended."

I looked at Carlos. He? My tech person was a she. "By Elizabeth Winstrop?"

"Elizabeth says you have someone very good."

I waited for Carlos to ask more about J'Leah Dawkins. He didn't. Carlos was still standing as if the band were breaking up, so I rose from my chair and said, "So we are agreed on the parameters of the check I've given to you?"

Carlos nodded. We signed some digital documents and he sent me copies. Then he held out his hand. "The documents are done, but no deal should be final until the hands have been clasped."

We shook.

Carlos moved back behind his desk. "I want you to prove there's nothing missing. The facility is secure. No one has had unauthorized access."

"You know that it's difficult to prove a negative."

"Look, Mr. Flint, I'm not asking you to find Russell's teapot."

Huh. We were back to Mr. Flint again. And I wondered if the teapot reference was a challenge or just Carlos' education showing through. I tucked my notepad away. "Modus tollens. If I don't find anything, that doesn't prove the negative. If there's a tiny teapot in orbit somewhere between the Earth and Mars, it'll probably stay hidden."

Carlos let loose a long laugh. "I knew I would like you, Jackson. I think we'll get along nicely."

3

MY OFFICE HAD THE BEST VIEW in town. That was by far its finest attribute.

Yellow Springs is a funky little village that remembers the sixties but doesn't dwell on them as its only source of peculiarity. We are as a community outspoken, strong-minded, friendly, insular, and stubborn—but man, what a great vibe. It seems like everyone wants to come here to hang out, slow down, and soak up the busking, arts, shops, nature, biking, coffee shops, and cuisine.

It's also a bit of a step back in time. There is no fast food. We have a local market, people walk and bike and sit on the benches downtown, and the eateries are local and family-owned. The tavern dates back to 1827.

My office window sits over the heart of it all. There's room in there for me, a small desk and chair, a filing cabinet with a coffee pot on top, and not much else. Visitors usually sit in a folding chair. The place is hard to find, with an entrance in an alley through a door that disappears into a mural painted on the wall. Then it's up a narrow staircase that twists into a maze of hallway. The door to my office is hung backward and blocks the way in when it's open. You have to close the door, step past, and reach back to open the door again and come in from the other direction.

The landlord had offered to fix the door, but I declined. I figured if anyone went to that much trouble to find me, they must really want to see me.

It was a warm September day and my window was open. Across the street someone was playing trombone solos on the steps in front of Tom's Market. A dark and musky tremolo wafted up. The tremolo broke to a quick jazz riff. Add a couple more brass, and they could have a New Orleans second line. Right here in Ohio.

I picked up my phone and touched a contact.

J'Leah answered on the first ring. "Jackson, what did I tell you about calling?"

"People don't do it anymore."

"Something like that."

"We're doing it."

"I make an exception for you."

I couldn't always tell how much was tease and how much was true. J'Leah usually answered when I called.

She said, "What's that sound?"

"Sound?" I held the phone out and listened.

"Where are you?"

"In my office."

"That probably explains it. Do you hear something?"

"You mean the trombone?"

"Trombone?"

"It's a brass instrument. Long sliding tube that allows for a lot of glissando. Popular in—"

"Put me on video call."

I sighed and touched some icons. J'Leah came up on video on my phone, her dark face and jet-black hair, smiling from what looked like an office desk staged in front of some sort of makeshift closet. I said, "You and your fancy technology."

"Jackson, this is not fancy. This is pedestrian. If it's on your phone, it's not fancy technology."

I tried to make out the images behind her. "Where are you?"

The angle shifted. A concrete wall and a single high window appeared behind her. "Work."

"Looks like a Faraday cage."

"Very good, Jackson. You're not as old as I thought."

"Actually, the Faraday cage is really old. Benjamin Franklin predated Faraday's demonstration by—"

"Stop now. Too old, too geeky."

"At your service."

She laughed. "Hold your phone out the window. I want to take in some of that Yellow Springs vibe."

Well, it beat a Faraday box in a concrete building. I slid the window screen up and leaned out, the village opening under me on the street below. I put J'Leah on speaker and angled the phone toward the trombone player across the street.

Her tinny voice came back through the window to me. "Is that a Christmas song?"

I listened. It sounded like *We Three Kings*. I spoke in the direction of the phone I held out the window. "Yeah."

"It's September."

"Maybe he's practicing." I retreated back into the office and closed the screen. The trombone shifted to *Raindrops Keep Falling on my Head*. It was a clear blue sky. I didn't comment on that.

The video feed tightened on J'Leah's face. "You're really living the life."

My mind skipped to Marzi and Cali, my girlfriend and daughter, then to the wheat penny and Quando. Yeah, the life, but some things could be a little sweeter. "I'm doing all right. I called about the job."

"The Drummond Brothers."

"Carlos and Drummond DeLuna. Drummond Brothers was a beer. My daddy drank it when I was a kid."

"OK, DeLuna brothers. Please don't tell me any more about the beer."

"Deal."

"They checked out?"

"We'll be working with just the one. Carlos." I left out the details.

"Carlos checks out?"

"Seems to. We met today. That's why I'm calling. We signed. It's a go. I'm going to need you to do your wizardry." We'd sketched things out before. I'd just been waiting to pull the trigger before I call J'Leah.

J'Leah took herself off video on the call. "What have you got for me?"

"Everything. Notes, photos, links."

"Uh-huh."

"It's a little unusual." We'd talked about that. It was why I'd waited to meet with Carlos.

J'Leah said, "I'd expect nothing less with you."

"Check out the background on these guys I'm going to send you. One of them is a genius, and the other seems to be some kind of sales guru."

"Noted. Got them. They look like brothers."

"I haven't sent you anything yet."

"Jackson..."

J'Leah had served a couple of hitches in the Marines, same as Brick. They bonded over it. And like Brick she'd come out with mad skills and a little trouble adjusting to civilians. J'Leah was lean and fast and strong and had tech skills I couldn't understand even if I'd had clearance. And she had a way of knowing things.

I pushed on. "Carlos is older by a couple of years. They do look similar." I heard a blur of mumbling and some clicking and typing. That meant J'Leah was already working.

"Send everything. I'll ask if I need anything else for the tech check."

"I'll email it."

She laughed.

"What?"

"Civilians. Email."

"If it's too tricky for me, I'll print everything and have it delivered secretly inside a pizza box."

She laughed again. "In that case, I'd like sausage, peppers, and extra cheese."

"No, it would just be the files in the box, no pizza—"

"I get it."

"And that stuff will kill you."

"The peppers?"

"Sausage and extra cheese."

"Maybe. But it'll take about seventy years."

"Listen, I'll just send the email."

"I think that's for the best."

There were more sounds of J'Leah typing fast. "You taking Brick? On the ground check?"

"Hadn't planned to."

The connection went quiet.

"I can handle it on my own. I assume he's got things to do."

"Why would you assume that?"

Good question. Brick and J'Leah both seemed to have steady sources of income, and J'Leah had hinted at some kind of job that I'd apparently just gotten a glimpse of, but exactly how those two got by was a bit of a mystery. And neither of them seemed to want to share many details. Maybe that was part of having served in special ops. It did something to people.

I pushed on again. "It's a fairly straightforward security check. I've done the prelims already—background on the company, titles and property records, degrees these guys earned in Mexico. The point is that I shouldn't be able to get into the compound. If I can't, that'll prove the point."

She was quiet.

"J'Leah?"

"Just be careful. I've seen things go sideways."

Sure she had. "I will. But hey, this isn't the Middle East. And it's not—wherever you served."

"Just remember."

The prime directive. J'Leah knew. We'd talked about it. "I'll be safe."

She ended the call. And that was that. When J'Leah was satisfied, she just disconnected.

I set my phone down and leaned on the sill to take in some more of the autumn air. The trombone busker had switched to something slow and bluesy. Lots of glissando on the transitions. I imagined sepia tones and dark windows with the shades drawn. Noir wafting up to the P.I.'s window. Cool.

I'd given Carlos a four-day window. I would do the check within four days, but I wouldn't tell him which one. The deal was that the staff knew there would be security checks, but they wouldn't know when.

Only Carlos and I knew the window. That would allow the others to be vigilant but not exactly tipped off. My thinking was that they wouldn't expect it right away. That's why I was going tonight.

I went home to get some things ready.

At five o'clock Cali came home. She was in her junior year of high school. In her head she was way ahead of that. Some of her friends were seniors, and she'd already started missing them even though they wouldn't be gone for another year. It didn't help that some of Cali's friends were taking college courses on the local campuses this year and she wouldn't see them at the high school as much.

I heard Cali call for the cat. "Mrs. Jenkins, where are you?" She whistled once.

Mrs. Jenkins was with me, in the bedroom where I squatted in front of the gun safe in the closet. "In here."

Cali appeared at the door. Her blonde hair hung to her shoulders and was washed out by the summer sun. She was tall for her age and had her mother's build, lean and compact.

Mrs. Jenkins looked at Cali. Cali looked at me opening the gun safe. "She doesn't know what you're doing."

Cali meant the cat. I sometimes had the feeling that Mrs. Jenkins was asking me if I was sure I knew what I was doing. Did I really want to carry the gun?

Cali tipped her head and her hair tilted down. "She's not mom, you know."

I knew.

Then Cali turned away. Mrs. Jenkins twitched her tail.

I pulled the Smith & Wesson M&P40 from the safe and tucked it into the backpack I had prepared. Then I went to Cali's door and knocked.

From the other side, she said, "You know the rule."

I did. The rule was that the door should stay open a few inches when she was inside on her phone or computer. But the rule had weathered poorly over the summer. I didn't think it would hold up much longer.

The door was barely open a crack now. I spoke through the gap. "I thought we could have a nice dinner together tonight."

There was quiet. The door opened. "Can we invite Marzi?"

"I'd like that, but it's not the best night. I have to work later."

"I noticed."

She meant the gun. "It's just a precaution. I'll leave it locked in the truck."

Cali's eyes drifted down. "You know that's why she won't come over here."

"No." I felt my head moving back and forth. "It's more complicated than that. Marzi will come over. We're just not ready…"

There had been some bumps over the summer. Sometimes I got roughed up a little in my work. Everything else seemed okay, but Marzi couldn't quite square her feelings about the inherent potential for danger in what I did. I thought there was more to it. She also couldn't square her feelings about my inherent potential to do what had to be done. Was I a nice guy with a violent streak that was justified, or was there something more going on?

It didn't help that Marzi was my former counselor. She'd worked with Cali and me when Kat died. When I lost a wife and Cali lost a mother. Throw that into the mix, and the whole thing with Marzi and me and Cali had a lot of room to get complicated.

"We can ask Marzi to come over tomorrow night."

Cali slumped back onto her bed. "What's the point? It's like you two are just friends anyway."

She knew it wasn't true. It was a weird paradigm. I wanted Cali to be careful about sex, and she was pressuring me to be more aggressive about it. "Marzi and I are more than friends. We're just taking some time to figure out where things are going." It was half true. I knew where I wanted things to go. Marzi was a little unsure.

Cali picked up her phone and turned away. "Suit yourself."

I stood in the doorway for a moment. Kat and I used to do that together, stand at her door and watch Cali happily go about the business of being a child.

It doesn't take long for things to change. Cali had been so good when Kat died. Strong and self-sufficient. Now things were more difficult. I knew some of it was Cali growing up, but Marzi re-entering the scene had changed the dynamic. From grief to yearning to lack of patience and disappointment.

"I got mung bean sprouts. I'll make fried rice." It was one of her favorites.

Cali's phone came down a tick and revealed her eyes. "It's not fair."

"I assume you don't mean the dinner?"

The roll of her eyes told me she didn't. And Cali was right. A lot of things weren't fair. It wasn't fair that she'd lost her mother. It wasn't fair that I'd lost my wife. It wasn't fair that Cali had to take care of herself while we adjusted to the loss. It wasn't fair that her friends were going away to college before her. It wasn't fair that Marzi hadn't moved in and made us a whole, happy family again.

There would be more unfair things to come. Things were unfair for everybody. It was only a matter of degree. But I knew that in this moment, one unfairness rose above all others for Cali: Marzi. It was for Cali as if the whole world revolved around this one thing, right now.

Cali toed a circle on the floor in front of her. "I miss mom."

It had been a while since she'd said it.

The toe circled some more. "When Marzi's here, I don't think about it as much."

Ouch. "I understand that. But can we at least have one nice dinner tonight, just the two of us? There will be time for things with Marzi later."

She shook her head. "I'm not hungry."

"You're always hungry."

"Dad!"

The grin gave her away. I pointed to the kitchen. "Thirty minutes."

4

I DID THE GATE CHECK at six-thirty. It was broad daylight, just after the close of regular hours. Nothing threatening.

I figured it to be easy-peasy. I show up, I'm not supposed to be there, they send me on my way. Just as things should be.

The perimeter check would come later. That might be a little more interesting.

I eased my old, black Silverado pickup down the back roads, under the trees and through the corn and soy fields, windows down enough to let the chill wind blow through the cab. An old Patsy Cline song fought to be heard against the rush of the air. I switched off the radio and left Patsy to her troubles, and in my head I went over my cover story again.

CDE Enterprises poked its head from the fields. Other than the fence around the buildings, it didn't look much different from the other old farms along the route.

I downshifted and turned onto the narrow lane. Dust followed me and settled around the truck when I stopped at the little guard shack by the entry gate.

An awning covered an intercom and digital screen on the side of the shack. A red light came on.

I lowered the window and leaned out to speak into the intercom. "Hello. Anybody there?" I smiled at the screen where I thought the camera would be and gave a casual wave.

The screen lit up and a message scrolled across. *Please wait. We will be with you in a moment. If you know the contact information for the person you are trying to reach, you may call or text now.*

I didn't call or text. I waited. A moment later, the screen flashed and the face of a man appeared. He was wearing a dark blue uniform and leaning over a desk. "Yes. Can I help you?"

"Thanks. I'm looking for my dog."

The quality of the video was good enough that I could see him blink. "Do you have an appointment?"

"No. I'm looking for my dog."

He blinked again. "Your dog?"

I stretched my arm out the window and lowered it down to hold my palm level a couple of feet above the ground. He probably couldn't see it, but I made a good show. "About this big. Mixed breed. A mutt. Brown and white and black. Good dog. He loves to chase things. He got away."

Instead of a blink I got a look of forced patience. "Your dog's not here."

"Listen, we just moved in down the road." I pointed vaguely. "Me and my wife. It's…okay, really we moved in with her sister-in-law. Things have been tough, you know? It's just until we get back on our feet."

If I had a miniature letterpress in the back seat I could pretend I was Jim Rockford, pretending he was someone else. Maybe I'd print a card that said I cleaned gutters, or trimmed your trees. Just a regular guy. Little down on his luck, trying to get by. Everyman charm. Looking for his dog.

But I was no Jim Rockford. And the guy wasn't buying.

I tried again. "So me and Ruffers—that's my dog—we go out just, you know, have a little time to ourselves. You know how it is? Mister, have you ever had a wife and a dog?"

Still no reaction.

"So Ruffers is new to the area, like me, and he run off. He's adventurous. He likes people and things. I thought he might have come here."

The face moved closer to the camera. "Your dog's not here."

"Ruffers digs. Did I say he likes people?"

"You did."

"What's your name? Mine's Johnny Jenkins."

"You can call me Daryl."

It didn't sound like his real name, but I went with it. "Daryl, can you let me look around? Call my dog?" I whistled once, long and trill, and called "Ruffers!"

"Mister, your dog's not here."

I leaned into the screen. "It's Johnny. Look, I don't know if you've ever had a dog. This dog—let's just say he better live forever, because I don't want to be alive without this dog."

"I understand." It didn't sound like he meant it. Daryl backed away from the camera.

"Wait. Can you give me your number? Can I call you later and see if Ruffers shows up?"

"I can't do that."

"Are you sure I can't just come in for a second and look? I'll whistle. If Ruffers is here, he'll come." I whistled once to show him what I'd do. "Here, Ruffers."

"I can't."

"I'll give you my number. You can text me if you see him?"

The man shook his head. "You can check back here later if you want. But I don't think we'll see him."

I hung my head and tried to look as pitiful as possible. "Thanks, Daryl. You're a good man." I lifted an eye to see if Daryl had softened.

He hadn't. So I stepped on the clutch and pushed the stick into reverse and very slowly started into a three-point turn and inched away from the perimeter fence and the entry gate and the empty guard shack.

The guy had done his job. He was probably more patient than I would have been. When I was a deputy with the county, pushing back on curious gawkers had been one of my least favorite parts of the job. This guy hadn't let me pull him out to the gate and away from his station, and he didn't give me his number. Either of those would have opened leverage, a guard out of position or distracted, or a contact to come at this again from another angle. The name Daryl probably wasn't even real.

It felt like a Patsy Cline song. I'd gotten nothing. I didn't even have a dog.

In terms of the security check, this was just the beginning. But so far, so good.

I drove away into the sun. I had a paperback Lawrence Block mystery novel in the glove box and a coffee from Dino's Cappuccinos in the cup holder. Block had been a local guy back in the day, and some of his stuff was a not-so-well disguised version of the village landscape. I headed for a little park on River Road to pass some time with the Canada geese who liked to float on the water there.

The park was quiet. I opened my paperback. Neither Block nor the geese disappointed.

When the sun was slanting low, I drove to a little ungated cemetery that looked like it hadn't seen much action since the settler days. The grounds were weedy and the trees were thick with low-hanging limbs and leaves. I tucked the truck under a tree in the back.

Then I thought about the M&P40 locked in the gun safe beneath the seat. The black truck had already almost disappeared in the deepening shadows. The weapon probably wouldn't be compromised if I left it in the truck. So why did I bring the gun if I wasn't going to carry it?

I looked out over the quiet gravestones. Those voices in my head were Brick's, Cali's, and Marzi's. Where was my voice?

The chatter cleared and my own voice whispered to me. I tucked the gun and clip into the backpack and secured the zipper pulls with a carabiner.

Then I got out and walked.

It was a little more than a mile to the CDE buildings. I timed my walk to arrive at a copse of trees west of the compound just before the sun descended into nothing but an orange glow.

The narrow copse straddled a streambed that carved a winding path through the farm fields. I stepped off the road into the trees and followed the edge of the stream. The banks were steep and thick with honeysuckle and walnut. I picked my way through the thicket and stopped when I was aligned with the last of the sun behind me, pointing directly at the back line of the perimeter fence around the compound.

The corner of the fence nearest me was about twenty-five yards away through a field knee-high in soybeans. I could make that walking quickly in about a dozen seconds. Half that time if I was running. I would be coming with the last rays of sunlight directly behind me. That might get me some extra time if there was a camera at this angle looking into the wash.

I ambled out in a medium-hurry.

No bells had gone off or horns sounded when I reached the high fence. No vehicles steamed across the compound toward me.

I sat by the fence with the soy plants around me. For show, in case a camera was picking me up, I pretended to be very tired and looking around for something. My dog Ruffers. Here Ruffers. Come on, boy.

It didn't take long for the field to darken completely. Long shadows stretched across the ground and seeped away. Still no one came and no alarm sounded.

I waited a little more for the darkness to deepen and my pupils to widen. I had my eye on a shallow and narrow drainage swale up the fence line. The swale extended under the chain-link and into the compound. Probably leftover drainage from before the fence was built.

I walked in the dark along the perimeter fence, still putting on some pretense of looking for my dog. It was probably too late to sell that now, but it was the cover story I'd built and I was sticking with it.

The swale was dry, as it should be on the early cusp of autumn. In another season it might have water or mud or snow, but now only weeds stretched up to cover the five or six inches that separated the ragged bottom of the chain-link from the bed of the swale. Not enough room for me to squeeze through. But enough for a dog to dig through.

I slipped off the backpack and reached in to extract the bit of rusty chain-link I'd clipped from an old garden fence at home. I stretched the jagged ends out into a makeshift trowel.

It was overselling it, I knew. The jagged wire approximated digging that a dog's claws might do. It was unlikely I could sell that to even the most naive buyer, and it was miraculous I'd gotten this far without being noticed by a human or a digital eye. I dug anyway. This is what I'd been hired to do, and this was how I was going to do it.

It went quick. The dusty ground gave way and the bottom of the swale deepened to a narrow trench under the fencing.

When the tunnel was deep and wide enough, I folded the bit of fence-trowel and flattened it and pushed it into the ground beneath a soy plant, with a twinge of guilt that it might get tangled in the farmer's combine if I didn't come back and get it later.

Then I bent the fence inward, as a dog would if it made the breach. That pointed the sharp ends away from me. I shoved the backpack through and pulled myself after it.

There was some satisfaction in it. I hadn't expected to get this far. It was probably imminent that I'd be picked up by a motion sensor or a camera.

I walked deliberately toward the enclosure that held the propane tank, as if I belonged there and had a task to do. Carlos had pointed out cameras around the front of the compound. I expected to see some here too, but I found none as I walked. That didn't mean they weren't there.

I cleared the propane station, and the farmhouse came into view. Lights shone through some of the lower-level windows and cast tic-tac-toe shadows over the ground. No one was visible, and nothing moved.

I didn't call for Ruffers. I walked straight to the farmhouse. A light clicked on above the door when I reached the step. I stood illuminated under the glowing dome and knocked loudly without hesitating.

More lights came on inside, and a vehicle started with a rumble somewhere near the front of the compound.

Beside the door, a digital screen like the one on the guard shack lit up and a voice drifted from the intercom beneath it. "Uhm? Yes?"

The man whose face appeared on the screen wore a white shirt and was cleanshaven. He looked like he should be wearing a pocket protector with various pens and pencils sticking out of it, but I guess that went out with the slide rule.

"I lost my dog."

"What?"

"I'm looking for my dog. Have you seen him? About this big." I held my hand out so it would be picked up by the camera. "Answers to Ruffers. Really friendly dog."

"Uhm?"

A vehicle moved toward me. Tires crunched on gravel.

"Are you supposed to be here?"

"Sure. I talked to the guy at the gate. I'm looking for my dog."

Headlights swept the ground.

I held up my phone. "Can you just come out and look? I have pictures. Maybe you've seen him."

"I'm not supposed to…"

The vehicle arrived. A gray SUV. I'd seen it parked by the entry that afternoon. The video screen went dark. I wasn't going to talk my way in. Good. I wasn't supposed to.

I turned and looked into the headlights. A figure emerged from the driver's side and crouched behind the door.

"Daryl? It's me, Johnny." It was worth a shot.

The tip of a pistol emerged over the open door where the window was down. "Hands up. Freeze!"

I put my hands up. "Slow down. I'm with the security check."

A second vehicle rounded the farmhouse and angled to a stop beside the first. Two men in uniform jumped out.

The first man stood from behind the SUV door and walked slowly toward me, gun locked in a shooter's pose. "Tom! I've got him."

Tom, who I recognized as the man who'd told me his name was Daryl, stopped, reached to a holster on his belt, released the snap, and raised his gun to me.

I shouted. "Wait. I'm with the security review. Check your weapons."

Nobody lowered a gun. The third guard had his up now.

The three approached, guns held high.

"Gentlemen. Slow down. I'm working with Mister DeLuna. I'm unarmed." Except I wasn't. The M&P40 was in my backpack. Maybe I should have listened more closely to the voices in my head.

Tom, who I suspected was the lead man, stopped directly in front of me. The other two flanked him a step behind.

I lowered my right hand a few inches. "I'm going to reach for my ID."

Tom pushed his weapon forward. "Keep them up."

I did. "Slow down. I was hired by Carlos DeLuna to perform a security check of the premises. That's what I'm doing. Let's dial this down."

Recognition flashed on Tom's face. "You're the guy from the gate."

"Yes—"

"Said you lost your dog."

"Yes—"

"That was a lie." He motioned to the man on his right. "Pat him down."

I stepped back, hands still up but farther apart, my back close to the farmhouse door. "If you'll just call Carlos. I'm sure he's briefed you."

The man who had been told to pat me stepped up and said, "Turn around."

I didn't. "There's been a mistake."

"Turn around."

I felt heat and adrenaline rising. I tried to tamp it down. This would get straightened out.

The man holstered his pistol and reached to a vest pocket and extracted a pair of zip ties. "Turn. Around."

I tried to fight it. But I felt that switch flipping open. I wasn't going to be bound. No way.

The man put his hand to my shoulder to turn me.

I knew it was wrong, but I was beyond that. I rolled in the direction of his push, whipped my right leg up behind me, and hooked the guard's legs and took him down hard.

There was no stopping now. Those guns had to come down—immediately. I came at Tom and the other guard low and fast and flung my arm around Tom's torso. I used my legs to drive him into the third man. Neither of them had so much as managed to lower his gun toward me before they dropped.

My senses were high. I had entered that weird dimension of time and speed like I was moving a frame faster and ahead of everything around me. It wouldn't last. I was already taking stock. One man down on the steps. Tom and the other man down and tangled but struggling for balance and control of their weapons.

I used that adrenaline to run.

It was two steps to the corner of the farmhouse. I dug my heel into the turn and put on the burners.

The far corner of the house flew by and I zagged left. Full tilt to the propane tank and around it.

Shouts and footsteps. A ringing in my ears as I ran faster. Sounds of a vehicle and then a gunshot.

Oh, hell no. They were shooting at my back? As I ran away?

I ripped the backpack off, threw it under the breach in the fence, and dived after it. The jagged wires at the bottom of the curled-up chain-link caught and bit into my neck. I kicked forward and the fence flexed and bit into the backs of my legs.

Then I ripped free and was up and running in the darkness, flying through the soybeans with the backpack tucked in my arm. I was The Freeze, the masked runner flying past fans racing on the warning track at a Braves game. Nobody could beat the Freeze.

No more gunshots sounded. No lights swept out over the field around me. No vehicles raced into the field in pursuit. I reached the trees and crashed through the brush into the streambed.

I ran in darkness through water and the tunnel of trees. Deeper into the fields, away from the road. Putting distance between me and the compound.

After an indeterminate amount of time, I stopped and listened. Maybe it was five minutes, maybe more. How far could I have gone in that time?

My neck and shoulders stung. I reached back and felt blood and ragged skin.

A vehicle sounded in the distance. Road noise, or from the compound? There were no sirens. Too soon, maybe. Or maybe the county cars would come silently. Or the CDE folks wouldn't call them at all.

The stream and the tree line took a sweeping turn here. There was larger debris, downed limbs, exposed rocks, logs crossing the water. I waded in and the water came to my thighs. Another step and it rose to my waist.

I backed out and climbed through the trees to the edge of a field. A house light shone in the distance, and another weaker light flickered farther away. A dim break in the terrain showed where a road might be.

I listened for dogs or cattle. I heard none. My eyes were adjusting to the moonlight. I was going to head where I thought the road should be.

I wedged my phone from my pocket. The screen was wet. I dried it on my shirt and made a call.

Brick answered on the second ring. "Mister Flint. Feeling manly?"

I sighed. "Not so much. Listen, can you do an extraction? The location's going to be a little tricky."

5

I TURNED ON THE LOCATION setting for my phone and a little blue dot on the map showed me that I had to walk a bit in any direction to get to a road. I chose a route that kept me away from houses.

I walked the edges of the fields following the trees and the stream. Eventually the stream would come to a bridge that crossed a road. That's where I would come out of the fields.

When I arrived at the place the blue dot showed, I was on a road but the road was unnamed. Now patches of grass and weeds grew up through the deteriorating surface and threatened to return the road to a more natural state. The dark outline of one old house loomed in the distance on each side of the byway, but I saw no lights or activity.

I walked the short distance to a larger named route and texted that location to Brick. Then I told him which direction I would be walking.

Right away I passed another old cemetery. This one was obviously no longer in use, with trees and brush grown over the site. No name remained on the wrought iron gate that hung loosely from an old post, but I could make out the edges of the weathered stone markers that hadn't yet fallen down. I hoped my recurring passing of cemeteries tonight wasn't an omen.

Brick texted. *OMW. ETA 12 min.*

That was oddly specific. I replied. *Walking your way.*

Then *ETA 8*. He was a precise kind of guy. Modern technology will get you that.

No other cars came from either direction until Brick arrived. I heard the Shelby before I saw the headlights swing through the turn ahead and come toward me. The lights slowed. I stepped into the road and raised my arms, and the lights flashed and approached.

The top was down. I was wet from the waist down, and part-way up. It was going to be a cold ride. I reached for the door handle.

"Hold up." Brick jammed the parking brake on and scooted up to sit on the edge of his door. He looked around in both directions. "No one's coming?"

I hadn't told him the whole story. Just that I needed an alternate way out. I reached for the handle again. "I'm clear."

"Hold up."

I did.

Brick was looking at me. He climbed out of the car and came around. Two fingers were up. "Two things."

I sighed.

"Your daughter is not going to like the way you look."

I looked down. My pants were wet and muddy. There was blood on my shirt and pants. I reached to my shoulder and felt the scratches and gouges from the fence on my back and arms.

One of Brick's fingers went down. "And you're not getting in the car like that." He motioned for me to turn around. I did. He pointed behind me to the backs of my legs. "That is going to make a mess."

I reached back. The sting when I rubbed my hamstrings reminded me what had happened there. "It's not as bad as it looks."

"Maybe. It doesn't look good."

"Nothing that needs stitches."

"Bad for the seats. What happened?"

I sighed again. "Can I tell you on the way?"

"Wait a second." Brick went to the trunk and pulled out a large, folded fabric thing and tossed that into the back seat.

"What's that?"

He unfolded the fabric and stretched it across the seat. "Dog seat cover."

"You don't have a dog."

He grinned really big. "Right. But Angelita's got one."

"Angelita?"

Brick closed the trunk.

I rubbed mud from my shoes. "From last summer?"

He nodded.

Angelita Rojas Flores had hired me to find out what was going on with an old family cabin in the woods she inherited. Things had gotten complicated, and Brick came in to help. Last I heard, Angelita had been angling for a ride in the Shelby. I guess she'd gotten it. Probably more than one.

I climbed onto the dog seat cover in the back. "So in this scenario I'm the dog?"

Brick got into the front. "Woof."

It beat walking. I gave him directions to the truck. He revved the GT and we rolled off into the night.

Brick shifted. "So?"

It was a question, but the wind was loud. I cupped one hand behind an ear.

He raised his voice. "Tell it."

I leaned to his ear and told it.

He listened all the way through, then asked a bunch of questions. He wrapped it up with one thing. "You're usually a careful guy."

"Heat."

He turned to hear better. "What?"

"Heat. I'm wet. It's cold and windy. I'm freezing back here."

Brick kicked the blower higher. "You want to put the top up?"

"No. We're almost there." I huddled toward the heat. Not much of it reached me. "I thought I *was* being careful."

"You got surprised."

I didn't like to admit it. But yeah. "It seems that Carlos hadn't notified the troops."

"You think that was on purpose?"

"I thought it was just unusual. But now...?"

"Maybe you surprised them by busting in on the first night. Or getting in at all."

"I'm starting to think there's more to it."

"It's not OK what the guy did to you. He put you in serious risk."

I'd downplayed the scene with the guns. But a gun was a gun. When one came out, that changed the whole scenario.

Brick slowed and made a turn. "Guy did that to me…" He didn't have to finish. I had a pretty good idea what he'd do.

I felt something hot start to smolder behind my temple. "I need to have a very serious talk with Mister DeLuna tomorrow."

"That's not all you're going to have to do tomorrow. You want me to follow you home and help you get cleaned up?"

I leaned forward so he would hear me clearly. "Why would you do that?"

He tilted the rear-view mirror and invited me to look in it. I couldn't see much from the back. He turned the mirror back. "You look a mess."

"Now I'm not following you. You want to help me get cleaned up?"

He shouted. "No. Interference." Brick glanced at me in the mirror. I couldn't have given him a blanker look. He said, "Cali's going to ask what happened. If she sees you."

"You want to give me cover?"

"Well, I promised."

"You promised Cali you'd help try to keep me out of trouble. It's too late for that."

"Then I can at least help try to cover it up."

Huh. "How are you going to do that?"

"I don't know. Come in and make tea? You could sneak in and clean up."

"Tea?"

He shrugged.

"What in hell are you talking about? I have never in my life seen you drink tea of any kind. If you showed up tonight and had tea with Cali, she would know for sure something was wrong."

"I guess."

"That would freak her out more than anything I've ever done."

"Sorry."

"I think I can talk to my own daughter."

"I said I was sorry."

I leaned back. "OK. Me too. It's not been a good night."

"Seems so. You have a change of clothes in the truck?"

"No."

"Towel?"

"No." I looked at the backpack. I had nothing useful there. "If I was a dog, you could take me down to the river and dunk me."

"If you were a dog I'd do that."

We slowed as I tried to point out the secluded entry to the cemetery where I'd left the Silverado. Brick found the turnoff and wound around the headstones to the truck. "Look, I don't know what I was thinking about Cali. She's a big girl. She's growing up."

"It's OK."

"I guess I just—been thinking about it, with Quando and all."

"I know." I grabbed the backpack and climbed out. "You want me to fold up the dog thingy for you?"

"Nah. Leave it there. Angelita might still be up."

I tried to give him a knowing look.

"She likes a little late-night ride in the Brickmobile."

"I'll bet she does."

Then he turned the Shelby around and bumped out of the cemetery. When he hit the blacktop road, the engine revved and the Shelby streaked off into the night, lonely and dark, like a scene out of *Two Lane Blacktop* or *American Graffiti*.

I turned to the truck. In the dark, there among the gravestones, I felt completely alone.

6

THE MORNING OFTEN BRINGS a fresh perspective. More clarity, a little optimism, an easier path forward.

The next morning brought a different perspective for me, but it wasn't brighter. I woke with Carlos DeLuna in my sights.

Contrary to Brick's concerns, Cali had barely noticed when I'd come home the night before. She'd been in her room, the door open an inch, her fingers working on the screen of her phone. It's what young people did these days.

I showered, cleaned up the wounds, and taped bandages on the worst of them. I threw away my ripped shirt and pants and the dirt and blood stains with them. It seemed petty, but I thought about putting the clothes on the expenses I would charge Carlos for the case.

I'd tapped on Cali's door to wish her a good night, poured a whiskey that I drank in the kitchen, then gone to sleep.

Mrs. Jenkins woke me before daylight when she thumped onto the bed. I reached to rub her ears. She let out a low, strangled growl. I knew that sound. Mrs. Jenkins had a full vocal range, mostly reserved for when she wanted a human to do something for her, or when another cat got too close to what she thought was her territory. But this particular sound meant only one thing: the growl was guttural and restrained because she was holding something in her jaws.

I rubbed my palms over my temples. This had been Kat's job. She would try to save whatever critter the cat brought in, usually a mouse or a vole. If it was beyond savable, Kat would shush the cat outside with its catch.

Mrs. Jenkins opened her jaws and a mouse plopped onto the bedspread. You want to miss your wife for more than this, but I really wanted to give the cat to Kat right now. I scooped up Mrs. Jenkins, and Mrs. Jenkins scooped up the mouse she'd just dropped.

I carried the cat to the window, lifted the screen, and gave her a nudge out. She plopped down into the plants.

Mrs. Jenkins had come to us feral, and sometimes it seemed she was still deciding if she preferred domestication or the wild. When she couldn't decide, I just put her out. Easy-peasy. Come back when you've settled down. I wondered vaguely if teenagers could be handled in a similar manner.

In the bathroom I checked the wounds on my legs and looked in the mirror at what the fence had done to my back. The itchy pink lines were already starting to scab over. I wouldn't put any more thought to them.

There were several things I would put thought to. Where was Carlos DeLuna? And why hadn't he contacted me after he learned what had happened last night?

And why hadn't I heard sirens?

I took my phone out onto the front porch deck and placed a call.

Bronigan answered on one ring. "Jackson."

"Bronigan." Roger Bronigan was a deputy with the county sheriff's office. He'd started just before I left. That was some time ago, and Bronigan still seemed to be stuck trying to work his way up the food chain.

Bronigan said, "You sound surprised."

"I didn't expect you to answer."

Now Bronigan sounded surprised. "Why not?"

"I figured with a new baby you'd either be trying to sleep, or sleeping."

"Henry is six months now."

"Time flies."

"You'd think so. In some ways it does. He's getting bigger. But it feels like the needle on when I won't have to change diapers again hasn't moved at all."

"When it's over, that will seem like it went by quickly too."

He grunted.

"You have a minute? I don't want to hold you up if you're getting ready for work."

"I'm still at work."

"What?" I'd called his personal number. "I thought they were going to move you off the night shift."

If it was possible to hear a shrug over a phone connection, I probably would have heard one. "It's back and forth. And I'm picking up some extra hours when I can."

"That doesn't sound good for someone with a six-month-old."

Bronigan laughed. "You know it, I know it, and Molly knows it. Tell it to my boss."

I remembered how it was. That's why I'd hung my own shingle outside the office door downtown. "And how is Molly?"

"Happy and proud mother. But she sure thought after that last thing we did I'd get a bump and a better shift."

I had met Bronigan in the summer when I was working the case for Angelita. There were loose ends that weren't tracking down. He'd done a thing or two that might not be exactly office protocol, and I had tried to return the favor by giving him a tip on a breaking case.

Bronigan's voice dropped a level in volume. "You didn't call just to chat."

"Wish I had."

"Let me have it."

"I'm interested in an event that happened last night. Wondering if it was called in. Clark County."

"That's not us."

"But you can check."

"You know I can."

"And that's why I called." I gave him the address and named CDE Enterprises.

"Give me a sec." There was the sound of typing. "That one came in. Two units responded. Intruder and break-in at the property. Long report. There'll be a follow-up."

I flipped my little notepad open on the patio table. "What time did the call come?"

More sounds of typing. "First call came at ten fifty-eight."

I wrote that down. "Eleven pm?"

"Twenty-two fifty-eight."

That was at least an hour after it was over. Huh. "You said *first* call."

"Right. That was from the address in question. Second call was from a neighbor a few minutes later."

"Later?"

"Said there were lights and cars in the soybean field. They thought it might be kids. Wanted someone to come check it out."

It wasn't kids. It was the security team, looking for me in the fields. An hour after I'd been gone.

"Jackson?"

"Yeah?"

"Something here interest you?"

"It does."

"Anything you can share?"

"That report came a bit later than I'd expected you to say."

"Is that interesting?"

"It could be."

When I didn't answer quick enough, Bronigan said, "What's your play in this?"

"I don't know that I'm entirely at liberty to say."

A breath. "You called just to find out if it was called in? You don't want to know anything else?"

"Can you tell me anything else?"

There was a quiet moment. I assumed Bronigan was reading from a report, or a preliminary report. "I don't know that I'm at liberty to say."

"Touché."

"But while we're here, what else might be useful for you to know? If I could tell you something?"

"A car was dispatched?"

"It was."

"At eleven o'clock?"

Another brief pause. "A unit arrived at twenty-three thirteen. A report was taken. No intruder was found or detained."

"Interesting."

"You keep saying that. I assume at some point you might be able to tell me why this is so interesting?"

"I hope so." I tapped my pen, thinking. "You want me to keep you in the loop on this in case there's something you can use?"

"Always. If I knew what we were talking about."

"And Bronigan? Take care of yourself. Give my best to Molly."

That ended the call.

The more I thought about it, the more unhappy I got with Carlos DeLuna.

I went in and put a kettle of water on to boil and dumped some grounds into the coffee press and sat down to chew on it some more. Instead of chewing, I stewed.

I went back out to the porch with a cup of coffee and ran through some tai chi moves to clear my muscles and the circuitry. I once took some lessons from a good man who thought it wasn't a good idea to do tai chi while overly stimulated. There is a move called raise the teacup. I put the cup of coffee on my palm and tried the move. I spilled the coffee. My teacher had been right.

I went in and refilled my cup, then went through some push-ups, pull-ups, and squats on the railing and framing timbers of the porch. The neighbors sometimes gave me funny looks when I did it, but it was handy equipment that worked in rain, shine, snow, or wind.

I was itching to call Carlos, but it was still early. I passed the time by doing something that always felt right. I went to the garden and picked an acorn squash. I cut that into slices and dropped those into a hot oiled skillet. I found an onion in the vegetable basket and part of a pepper in the refrigerator, and I sliced those and added them to the squash.

Then I mixed a thick biscuit batter of flour and yogurt and dropped spoonsful into another pan with oil. I took a can of black beans from the pantry and pulled eggs from the refrigerator.

The eggs were from a farmyard down the street. The chickens roamed the neighborhood and scratched for bugs. I think some of the kids had named the chickens, but I didn't know how you could tell one chicken from another unless they wore little nametags.

The eggs were sometimes dirty, like eggs that don't come from a supermarket are. I wiped straw and dirt away and wondered if the eggs had come from little Dottie or Delores or whatever names the kids had given them.

I read through a few more pages of the Lawrence Block novel while things cooked.

When the alarm on Cali's phone beeped, I went back and knocked on her door. "Breakfast."

She groaned. "It's just the first alarm."

I knocked again.

"I never get up on the first alarm."

"I know. That's why you never get a good breakfast."

Nothing but quiet came from the other side of the door.

"I'll make you a plate. If you don't have time to eat it, you can take it for lunch."

A groan erupted from behind the door. "Nobody takes their lunch."

"Then you'd better get out here and eat it for breakfast."

I retreated to the kitchen and arranged two plates with squash and peppers and onion, topped with black beans and an egg.

This wasn't my first rodeo. Cali might turn out for breakfast, or she might not. If she didn't, I might save her plate for her or I might not. I might eat that too. We both knew the lay of the land.

Cali came out a few minutes later, yawning, and sat at the little kitchen table.

"Coffee?" I gestured to the press. She was just beginning to drink a little splash now and then.

"Yes, please."

I put a dollop of cream into a cup and added a little coffee. Cali took that and stirred in a few grains of sugar.

I picked up my fork and held it in front of me. Cali did the same and we clicked forks.

"Cheers."

She yawned. "Cheers."

Clicking forks was something her mother had liked to do. I couldn't remember the last time Cali and I had done it.

Having successfully clicked, we dug in. She lifted the edge of her egg with a tine and looked under. What she saw seemed to suit her, and she squared off a forkful and took a bite.

I dove in more whole-heartedly. Biscuit, egg, squash, beans, coffee all at once.

Cali took another bite and a tiny sip of coffee. Then she set her cup down. "I'm sorry that I think I've been a little...something lately."

"Grouchy?"

She looked up.

"That's not what you were going to say?"

"No."

"Well, when you decide what the right word is, let me know."

She dropped her eyes as if in disbelief.

I tried again. "Maybe you meant to say...wonderful? Lovely? Intelligent and thoughtful?"

Now the twinkle came back to her eye.

I piled on. "Marvelous, stupendous, unflappable?"

"Those aren't things you apologize for."

"Nah, but they suit you."

Her face scrunched. "I don't think I'm unflappable. What does that even mean?"

I waved my arms like they were wings.

"Dad, you are so weird sometimes."

I shrugged. It hadn't killed me yet.

Cali arranged another bite on her fork. "I was going to say *grumpy*."

"Did you say *grampy?*"

"Grumpy."

We ate some more. I ventured out a bit onto a limb. "Anything you want to tell me about?"

"What do you mean?"

"What's been making you grumpy."

She gave me a look I didn't understand. I assumed that meant no.

A bite later, she set her fork down. "Things have just been different.

Sometimes I don't know what..." Her eyes went down like she wished she hadn't said anything.

I looked at my daughter. "It's okay. You're large. You contain multitudes."

She groaned.

"A wise man once said."

"I know who wrote it."

My fork stopped. "You do?"

"Well, you didn't read it on a Snapple cap."

"Snapple?"

She frowned. "What do you mean?"

"What's a snapple?"

"It's—never mind." She pushed her plate back. "I have to get ready to go."

I looked at her plate. There was enough still there to save for later.

Cali finished her splash of coffee. "Whitman."

I grinned like a kid with his thumb in the pie.

Cali got dressed and did the other things a teenaged girl did to get ready for school. When she came back out, I was finishing the dishes. She lingered for a second behind me while I dried.

I set the towel down. "What?"

"You said we could invite Marzi over tonight."

There must have been a question on my face.

"Last night. You said we would invite her tonight."

I guess I did. "We can do that. Weeknight, so it'll have to be something simple."

She looked at the squash rinds in the compost tray. "With you it's always something simple, but...not quite simple."

Fair enough. "OK. I'll ask Marzi."

I thought that was it, but Cali lingered. I looked at the clock. It was getting late. "Anything else?"

"What happened to your neck?"

"What?"

"And your legs?"

I was wearing shorts. I'd forgotten. I made an effort not to touch the wounds and draw more attention to them. "It's not summer if you don't have scratches on your legs."

She didn't buy it.

I tried a little honesty. "I got tangled in a fence."

Her frown deepened. "You were putting in a fence?"

"I had to climb under one."

I got the unhappy look.

I rubbed a hand over my face. "Some things didn't work out quite as I expected last night."

"What else?"

"What else what?"

"What else got hurt?"

"It's just some scratches. Nothing to worry about."

She lingered. Unhappy.

I said, "It's fine."

She still lingered. "Are you going to tell me?"

"It was a work thing that had a few wrinkles." I remembered the gunshot. That was more than a wrinkle. I felt guilty about it, but I said no more.

Cali's frown was still parked on her face. She finally turned away. "Will you at least cover up when Marzi's here?"

My answered was a nod.

When Cali had gone, I stewed some more. What the hell had happened last night? Then I put the towel down and let the dishes lay. I had a fish to fry, and its name was Carlos DeLuna.

7

A SHAKEDOWN wasn't my usual M.O. Neither was getting zip-tied or shot at in a soybean field, so I made an exception. I put on my game face and called Carlos DeLuna.

It went to message. I left one. "*Mister DeLuna.*" No more Carlos and Jackson. "We need to talk. I'm sure by now you know why. This will go easier if you tell me where you are. I don't want to have to look for you." My finger hovered over the call button. I moved it away. "I'll start at your office. I'm thirty minutes away. I won't want to wait."

I grabbed my jacket. My hand went instinctively to my belt. Habit. A deputy never goes on shift without his weapon properly holstered. But a P.I.?

It was the old debate. Safer with the gun or without. Asking for trouble or preventing it? Provoking or being careful?

I opted for comfort. I went back to the bedroom and the gun safe in the closet.

Mrs. Jenkins met me in the hall. Licking her paws. The last of the breakfast mouse. She looked at me like she was asking the question. Who you gonna shoot, boy? You really want to do this?

She swished her tail and walked away. Like my conscience letting me go. Letting me make my own choice, but with a stern warning that the angels and devils were looking over my shoulder. I ignored the cat and went for the gun.

In the truck, I worked the radio dial looking for motivational music.

Bee Gees. Nope. Lumineers. Nope. Travis Tritt. Not quite. Tom Petty. Bingo. He wouldn't back down, and neither would I.

The song ended and I was spinning the dial again when Carlos called. I touched the phone in its holder.

Carlos jumped in. "Jackson, I—"

"Mister Flint."

"I don't—"

"You can call me Mister Flint."

"I don't—"

"Mister Flint."

There was a pause and I heard only road noise and radio static. I turned the radio off.

Carlos found his words. "Mister Flint, I understand that you're upset." He paused.

"Go on."

"I believe there's been a misunderstanding." Another pause.

"Continue."

"I can explain. You don't need to come to me. I believe we can clear this up over the phone."

"Nope."

"I—what?"

"We'll talk in person."

"I can save you some time. Can you talk now?"

"Nope."

There was a brief gurgled sound as if Carlos cleared his throat. "I don't understand."

"We'll talk in person."

"That's not necessary."

"It is." I waited.

Carlos waited.

I said, "I hope there isn't another misunderstanding here."

"No, I think I understand. Let me just say that—"

"Ten minutes."

"What?"

"I'm ten minutes away from your office."

The gurgling sound happened again. "I can't be there in ten minutes."

"I'll wait. But not for long."

Some air escaped from Carlos. "I hope you'll hear me out."

"Sure thing." I ended the call and went back to the radio. Eye of the Tiger came through. Yup, that would do.

At the lot in front of Carlos' building, I waited in the truck for five minutes. I was starting to mellow and I didn't want that. You can't do a proper shakedown if you're not feeling it. I should have brought Brick. He could stand in the corner and cross his arms and say nothing, like the big silent guy in the Ken Kesey book. A little crazy goes a long way in the intimidation game.

But I didn't have Brick. All I had was me and the Smith & Wesson. And it hit me that the gun wasn't the kind of muscle I wanted to bring to this party.

I slapped my weapon into the gun safe in the truck and walked to the building. My shoulders felt tight and I hunched them and twisted my neck to get the kinks out. Loose. Ready. How did Bogie do this in the movies?

I opted for leaning against the wall outside of Carlo's office door. If I'd had a fedora, this would have been the place to tip it down over my eyes.

I didn't have to wait long. And it turned out I didn't have to be Bogart. Carlos came alone, and he was very nervous. He rushed down the hall when he saw me.

"Jacks—Mister Flint, I am sorry that I'm late." He fumbled a key into the door. "I understand that you are upset. The men, they didn't expect you."

"That's the problem." I followed him into the office.

Carlos moved quickly behind his desk and showed me that he had his phone in his hand. "I believe that we can settle this, but I will not hesitate to call for help if that's necessary."

I stood over his desk, crossed my arms, and said, "Please do."

He blinked. "I beg your pardon."

"Please do. Call whoever you like."

Carlos sat frozen like a canary with a hawk circling.

I said, "You'll call 911? Your men?" I tipped my head back to the open door. "There is no building security here."

Carlos sagged.

"And what will you say? It was you who screwed up here."

The canary found his backbone. Carlos straightened. "It was you who fucked up, Mister Flint."

I uncrossed my arms, pulled a chair carefully up to Carlos' desk, and sat across from him. "Is that another word you learned in the old country?"

"No. This word I learned here in your country. We have many colorful words in Spanish for expressing emotion. But this word I reserve for special occasions. You fucked up. You attacked my men."

"They drew their weapons."

"That is what security does."

"They didn't know I was coming."

"A security check will go better if it is truly a check."

"That's not what we agreed to."

"You said four days."

I held up four fingers on one hand. Then I folded one down so three remained.

Now Carlos put up a hand, patting the air. "Mister Flint, what is it that you want?"

"I don't like being shot at."

His eyes widened. "Gunshots?"

I made a gun with my fingers and mimed *Pow*.

"This…" Carlos shook his head. "I did not know about the gunshots. It was not meant to be so serious. This was to be a simple thing. I must apologize. Let me call and ask about this." He lifted his phone.

I put my hand over his and stopped him. "Later." I didn't believe him. His team should have briefed him by now.

Carlos looked shocked that I'd touched him. "Of course." He put the phone down.

We looked at each other.

Carlos said, "And what now?"

"I don't think you ever intended to tell your people that I was coming. I want to know why."

He patted the air again, still searching for something. "No. We did not expect you so soon. You surprised them."

I shook my head. "Why were three guards working that night?"

Carlos' eyes shifted.

"You said there are three guards. They work in shifts. Three were there last night."

"To prepare. To be briefed. You arrived before that happened."

"Why was the incident not reported to the sheriff for more than an hour? If your men hadn't been briefed, they should have called it in right away."

Now Carlos' eyes flitted as if searching for something. "The neighbors. We try to keep quiet. It became necessary to alert the authorities."

I didn't like the way his eyes moved. I didn't like that his answers were slick. I didn't like that I felt myself softening. "You wanted to keep it quiet."

"Yes. You were not supposed to get in. Mister Flint, you are too good. You eluded my men. You bettered them. They were not prepared for someone of your caliber."

Flattery will get you somewhere. I knew that game. I was fighting not to soften, but I was losing. Some shakedown. I was no Bogie, fedora or not.

"Mister Flint—I regret not calling you Jackson. Mister Flint, things got out of hand. Mistakes were made. For that, I apologize. But this is not an insurmountable problem. I am prepared to compensate you for your, uh—unexpected troubles."

"You've already paid me."

"It will be doubled."

"For me to walk away."

He fidgeted. "I'll um—your specialist. The cyber check. I'll still want something."

"I think that's off the table."

"It can be rather…pro forma. A simple look. A brief report. Enough to be convincing for a potential buyer."

I stood.

"Mister Flint."

I pulled out my phone. "Mister DeLuna, do you have children?"

His eyes came up, confused. Then he focused. "A daughter and a son. Josephine and Tanner."

I swiped my phone to a photo and held that out. "My daughter. Cali." She was sitting in a porch chair at home, smiling like all the wattage of the world flowed through her. "If anything happens to me, she pays for it."

Carlos looked.

"I could have been shot. If something happens to me because you lied to me, you will pay for that."

His eyes said he understood. His mouth said, "I'll triple your pay. We still have a contract."

"The contract is null and void. False premises."

He pulled a checkbook from a drawer.

I leaned over his desk. "Why me?"

Carlos rubbed a hand over his temples.

"Why hire me for a job you didn't want done?"

I thought he wouldn't speak, but then his answer came almost in a whisper. "Elizabeth Winstrop."

"Elizabeth?"

"Yes. Because I had a connection to you. Because you were handy."

"You thought I'd be soft."

"It was to be a simple thing. A little briefing. A little drive-up."

I pocketed my phone and stood.

"Wait."

I almost didn't.

"I was embarrassed."

I turned back.

"I am still embarrassed."

I faced him.

"This whole thing is…with my brother Drummond. My wife Judy."

I waited.

"They don't know. No one knows. About Drum. His gambling. The risks. The breaches. The whole thing could come apart. All of it. We would lose everything."

I didn't like to watch a man cry. I didn't like watching Carlos cry. But his eyes leaked and he didn't try to hide it.

"I wanted to…I didn't want anyone to know. It's so awful. Judy didn't want anyone to know about the cancer. I didn't want anyone to know about Drummond and the trouble CDE is in. We haven't told anybody."

"You told me. About your wife."

"You are safe. No one knows you. You will come and go and keep your secrets. Your business cards say you are discreet." Now he wiped an eye. "And I thought telling you about Judy would convince you to take the case."

If he was acting, he was good. Or I was soft. Or both.

"It is just so terribly…" Carlos dropped his head. "Embarrassing."

I tried to get my feet to walk away.

Carlos clicked his pen and wrote the check. Like a fool, I waited while he pushed it across the desk.

"Mister Flint, I understand that you are hesitant. Let me apologize again for the misunderstanding. This has all been so terribly difficult. I didn't want anyone to know." He clicked the pen and slipped it into his shirt pocket. "Please consider this to be my earnest plea for you to complete the job. It need not be difficult. Something perfunctory, and a brief report. There will be no further risk for you."

I looked at the check. It had a big number on it.

"Take it. Whether you complete the work or not. Call this thinking money. Or apology money. Either way you like. You can walk away with this, or you can help a stupid old man who has made mistakes. Either way, the money is yours."

Interesting. I wouldn't want to play poker with this guy.

Carlos stood and bowed. "Whatever your decision, Mister Flint, I apologize to you for my transgressions."

Oh, damn. I pushed the check into my pocket. "I'll consider this thinking money. I'll let you know my decision."

Carlos tipped his head. "As you say."

I walked away. The sun was out when I reached the parking lot, and my mood had lightened. I wasn't sure what had just happened, other than a reminder that shakedowns weren't my strongest suit. But I had a big fat check in my pocket, so that was something.

8

"**YOU GOT PLAYED.**" J'Leah leaned over the porch railing at the Mills Park Hotel and looked north up into the village. "The guy is hiding something."

We'd just had lunch on the hotel porch at Ellie's restaurant. J'Leah had a double latte and the squash salad. I had the sweet potato bowl and picked up the tab. There were perks to getting paid triple for a job you didn't have to finish. I'd explained it all to J'Leah over the meal.

I leaned on the rail next to her and followed her gaze, up past Alan's castle, where an artist had lived and spent half a century painting portraits of villagers and tourists on the street and building and rebuilding an elaborate structure of bricks and glass and gardens. "You didn't have to come all the way out here to tell me that."

She waved an arm out over the village. "And miss all this? It's much better in person than with you hanging your phone out the window."

I laughed. "Most things are."

"At the very least, Carlos DeLuna isn't telling the truth. Or all of it."

"We agree on that." I checked the time, thinking about something else I wanted to do before dinner with Cali and Marzi. The last thing I wanted was to run late, seeing how things had been bumpy enough lately with my daughter and whatever label might apply to me and Marzi. What did the kids call it these days when you got together and then one of you wasn't exactly sure if you were a good fit? Or maybe I didn't want to know.

I tucked my phone back into my pocket. "What I haven't entirely decided yet is what comes next."

J'Leah raised an eyebrow.

I raised an eyebrow back.

"Jackson."

"J'Leah."

She shook her head. "Stop that. You know what comes next."

I leaned back. I do?

She was already making her way to the hotel steps and the street below. "Walk with me to your office. We're going to check him out."

We are?

I followed her. We passed some people holding phones up in front of the sloping and winding brick walls of the castle. The place housed a shop or two now and a pop-up store for the local celebrity. It was a popular spot for selfies.

We stepped into a streetside bed of mulch and flowers to get out of frame and avoid photobombing.

J'Leah smiled at the tourists. They smiled back. Three young women and a guy with them, all looking happy. J'Leah stepped back onto the sidewalk. "A girl could get used to a little town like this."

"Find yourself a nice boy to settle down with."

She shook her head. "A nice boy can find me to settle down with."

"Is that the way you kids are doing it nowadays?"

She looked over.

I grinned to show my intent.

"Jackson, are you trying to be funny?"

"You know, Brick asks me that same thing."

"That should tell you something."

"That you two don't know good humor when you hear it?"

"Keep thinking."

We passed the gas station and crossed Glen Street, then walked past the Sunrise Cafe, one of my favorite spots to eat, and home of the Jackson Flint breakfast special. I stopped to look at the menu written in chalk on the sandwich board out front.

J'Leah pulled my arm. "How can you be thinking about food? We just ate."

I shrugged. "I don't know. It just happens."

We sauntered past the salon, the theatre, and the flower shop. It was a clear fall day with a hint of cooler weather to come. A couple of people on bicycles slipped into the lane of cars on the main street. Someone walked a dog. A smattering of people sat on the benches outside of Tom's Market. We passed some diners taking a late lunch at the tables on the sidewalk in front of Current Cuisine.

It really was a little slice of paradise here.

We slipped between the buildings to the alley where the entry to my office was hidden. Something occurred to me. "I thought you had a job you had to be at?"

I got a blank look.

"You know, little cinder block room with a Faraday cage in it? Typing away and doing secret things on your laptop?"

She let loose an unladylike snort. "Jobs is another thing my generation does different from yours."

I laughed. I'd quit my pension job and hung my own shingle. Not so different from her generation. "You must be thinking of my daddy's time."

She laughed back. "Or your mother's."

I tipped my head. Touché. Some guy would be lucky to have J'Leah to settle down with, if she would have one. If she found my gender to be worth the trouble.

We followed the murals down the alley to the nearly invisible door that led to a maze of stairs and narrow hallways and then to my office. We did the dance around the door that was hung backward and stepped inside.

J'Leah went straight behind my desk and sat in my chair.

I stopped and unfolded one of the little chairs that leaned against the wall and sat across from her. "Comfortable?"

She pushed my laptop and empty coffee cup aside and tipped back in my desk chair to reach the window behind her. She pressed the sash up a few inches, and cool air wafted in. "Better." Then she unzipped the black backpack that was nearly always with her and took out a slim laptop computer.

I sank onto the creaky folding chair. "You probably still have the Wi-Fi password from when we worked out of here last summer."

She waved a hand and set her phone on the desk next to her laptop. "I'm going to want something faster." Then she reached into a pocket on the backpack and came out with a cable that she plugged into her phone and then her laptop. "And more secure."

I shrugged. That's why she was the expert.

J'Leah touched some things on her phone and her laptop and then lifted her hands from the electronics and leaned back. "Before we get started, you have the release?"

I held a finger up. "Before we get started with what, exactly?"

"This guy is hiding something. Let's poke around and see what we can find."

"I'm fine with that, but I just want to make sure you heard the part about we get paid whether we continue or not. We can stop now. And get paid in triple." Which we already had. The check was in the bank.

"I heard."

I waited. "But?"

"I'm interested. And you should be too."

"I'm interested. This has some unusual angles to it. Though I'm sort of not hired for the job anymore."

"And you're also sort of still hired."

"Like I said, angles."

She leaned forward. "We should at least take a preliminary look. See if there's any juice behind CDE's cyber security. A quick cut will show a lot."

I nodded, like I knew what she was talking about. "And what will that get us?"

"If the security is soft, we'll know he was never really serious."

"Or he's got a serious problem. Or something is going on."

J'Leah cracked her fingers and sprawled back in my chair, taking in the air from the window. "Your call. Guy did to me what happened to you, I'd want to know more about it if I could."

OK.

"I'd want to get even."

Uh-huh.

"You seemed pretty mad when you were telling me about it."

"I was."

She twisted her neck, getting comfortable in my seat. "I'd want to know what I might have been implicated in."

She was right. I opened my email on my phone. "To be clear before we do this, let's review. I've been hired by a client to do a security check for his business, CDE Enterprises, LLC, registered in the state of Ohio. That client has given me clearance to search for vulnerabilities in the cyber systems, releasing me from the federal prohibition on hacking and other such attempts at entering a secure cyber domain without permission. That client has also released you, though not specifically by name, as contracted by me, for the same purposes."

J'Leah stared. Then she grinned. Then she laughed. "Your lawyer give you that to read?"

"You've met my lawyer. He didn't give it to me."

She didn't look convinced.

I moved a hand across my chest in an x. "Cross my heart, it was all me."

"Well you sound like S.T."

Samuel Thomas was my lawyer. He'd helped me out of a jam that J'Leah had been involved with. "I'm sure he'd be disappointed to hear you say that."

She didn't quite grin. Instead she turned back to her laptop. "Send it."

I emailed the release form to her.

J'Leah took a few minutes to read it over. "You don't mind if I verify the digital signature?"

I'd been humming something I couldn't quite place. I waved a hand. "Of course."

J'Leah did some more things on her laptop and then looked satisfied. She looked back to me. "What are you doing?"

"What?"

"You're humming."

"I guess so."

"What is it?"

"What is what?"

"That you're humming?"

I worked out a line that was in my head. "Trombone Christmas carol, I think."

She shook her head. "This place is so weird."

I guessed so. "Where do we start?"

"Bonehead 101."

"Uhm…?"

"You understand this release also applies to the ORC?"

I didn't hide the surprise on my face. "J'Leah Dawkins, are you referring to section 4749 of the Ohio Revised Code of laws?"

"I am."

"Well color me impressed."

I got a look. "What? Color you?"

"It's an old people expression. It doesn't mean anything about your skin."

She looked at her dark brown skin and then my pale white complexion, and typed. "Googling it." She read the results. "Old people are strange."

I probably had her by a dozen years, at the most. "Why do people keep saying that?"

"Doesn't matter." She gestured to her screen. "This form also releases you to share client information with me as a third party."

"That's the point."

She gave me goggle eyes.

I gave them back to her. "What? Are we being extra careful here?"

"No." She pointed a finger at me. "I'm being the right amount of careful. I'm going to try to break into various aspects of the CDE servers. I probably won't get caught, or even noticed, for a long time. If ever. And I'll cover my tracks. But this is both a federal and a state crime if permissions aren't granted."

"Right."

"I'm thinking of both of us here."

J'Leah had her serious face on. OK, it was serious. I gave her my game face back. "You know I trust you."

She nodded and started typing. "Here we go."

"Bonehead 101."

"Uh-huh."

I picked up the thread of the trombone carol and started humming again. "You're going to try a sequel injection."

J'Leah's fingers stopped and her eyes came up.

"Trying to jack a password."

The typing started again. "So Jackson Flint has heard of SQL."

"Is that how you pronounce it?"

She didn't say.

I said, "You inject language to change information to instruction. Like a—"

She whistled and raised a hand. "Stop. Color me impressed."

"See? It's contagious."

Her fingers moved at high speed now. "There's no excuse for SQL injection vulnerability if you're serious about security."

She typed. Erased. Typed again. Tried a few more things. "OK, I'm not seeing vulnerability on the first volley. I'm going to try something else."

I waited.

She typed and swiped. "I'm looking for employee login pages or other web pages that might be dark." She looked me in the eye. A challenge. Did I want to guess what that meant, mister smarty-pants?

"You're looking at the html code for the page. Scanning for something that might reveal a page not linked in the visible text. A page that's there but you have to know what to type in the address to get it, or you have to have the link."

She sighed. Disappointed. "How do you know that?"

"I don't, really. I can scratch the surface. You're here to dig deep."

She didn't look happy.

"Carlos DeLuna wanted you. He knows your reputation. Somehow. He knew if he got me he could get you because..."

J'Leah was looking at me the same way I was looking at her. She tipped her head. "Does that seem like another odd angle?"

It did. "What's odd about is I don't think he knows your name."

"Go on."

"He just seemed to know that there was someone I'd worked with. I think maybe Elizabeth Winstrop told Carlos, but she may not have told him your name."

"She might not remember it."

I agreed. "He might be looking for someone who knows where to start trying to get in. The obvious places. Cover his bases, sort of."

"That all makes enough sense. But why go through the trouble? He hires you. That gets screwed up and you get shot at. He lied. Then he tells another story, with some truth to it—maybe. Then he fires you, sort of, and now he wants me to keep going?"

"Maybe he wants you to find something."

"You didn't find anything. You climbed right under the fence."

"I found that I could get in."

"OK."

"That seemed to surprise Carlos."

"Unless that's what he wanted—for you to get in."

I shrugged. "It didn't seem like they expected me. And I didn't get inside the farmhouse."

J'Leah pinched the bridge of her noise. "This whole thing could be nothing. It could be exactly like Carlos DeLuna said."

Neither of us was convinced.

J'Leah scanned her screen again. "So here's what we know. They pass bonehead 101. There might be vulnerabilities, but here's nothing that's front-page obvious. Their system may have some teeth to it."

"You think you can get in?"

"Maybe."

"Maybe?"

"There's a lot of different things to try here. I can phish for employee names and information. Someone who works there lists their job on LinkedIn, or something like that. I can set up a bot to search for the company name, jobs, associations, that kind of thing. That might lead to social media, or public documents like mortgages or sales or purchases of a property. And that could lead to someone who has an account somewhere that is vulnerable and has similarities in the password structure. And that's just for starters. There's also—"

"Stop." I held a hand up. "You're the expert. But I have one question."

"Uh-huh."

"Why exactly are we doing any of this if we've already gotten paid and we don't have to?"

"We've covered this."

"What's our net gain?"

She'd tapped a finger on my desk. "There's some reason this guy hired you. And there's some reason why you got the screws put to you. I thought you were still mad at this guy."

"I…am."

"You're not unhappy?"

"I am. I just…don't want any more trouble than I've already gotten."

J'Leah gave me a look I didn't like.

I stiffened. "Listen, I've got as much cajónes as anyone. But I also have a daughter. I don't want things to get any more sideways than they already have. We don't have a free ticket to try to breach mortgage websites for personal passwords. That's another can of worms. Any trouble for me is also trouble for Cali."

J'Leah and Cali had met. They got along. It was a good thing.

I said, "I don't know why I'm being so—capricious here. We should just do it. Lately I've just been thinking more about how my work is affecting my…"

I stopped. TMI.

J'Leah had a big grin.

"What?"

"Capricious?"

"It means—"

"I know what it means."

I held my hand out in surrender. "So sue me. I've been reading the dictionary."

"Uh-huh." J'Leah closed her laptop and pulled loose the cord that tethered it to her phone. "I get what you're saying about Cali. And I respect it." She reached for her backpack.

"So we're done?"

"If you want to be. We've already been paid." She stuffed things into her backpack. "But there's something wrong about this guy. He's hiding something. And I think you might be better off knowing what it is than not knowing. I don't think this has played all the way out yet."

It rang true with what I'd been thinking.

J'Leah zipped her backpack. "And he said he *wants* you to keep going. There's something very weird here."

There was.

"Plus, now I really just want to know."

"But you can't try to break into sites that aren't associated with CDE. We aren't covered for that."

"I didn't say it would be easy. It would be easier if it weren't illegal. I'll have to work around that."

I wasn't entirely convinced. But I trusted J'Leah. "How long?"

"There is no how long. It could be real soon. Could take a while. This guy has a deadline?"

"Wants a report within a week. Sooner the better."

"Then that's how long it'll take. Whatever we can find by then."

I got up and folded the little chair and leaned it carefully against the wall. "Do it."

9

I WASN'T GOING TO BE LATE. I promised myself that. I had told Cali I'd be there when she got home from school and we would start getting dinner ready for when Marzi came over.

But there was something else I wanted to do before that. I thought I could squeeze it in. I took out my phone and called Elizabeth Winstrop. There was an answer on the third ring.

"Jackson."

"Missus Winstrop. You've got caller ID."

"I couldn't *not* get it. This new phone."

"Well, I'm happy to know I've made your contact list."

"Ah. You assume I have a smart phone. A mobile."

"I do."

"You are correct. Having a teenager around will change your perspective on a great many things."

"I suppose it would."

"Willow has shown me the do not disturb function. Greatest invention known to humanity, as far as I can tell. With all due respect to Robert."

Her deceased husband. Robert had been the connection to the DeLunas. Willow Winstrop was the granddaughter Elizabeth didn't know she had until a series of unusual events after Robert's passing that Elizabeth had hired me to investigate.

"Cali said she's seen Willow at the high school. I assume your daughter Henna has stayed in the area?" That had been a tough one. Elizabeth and her daughter had been estranged for twenty years before I put them back together.

"Henna and Willow are, in fact, so much in the area that they are staying here in the house with me."

It was a big house. One of the biggest and oldest in the village. It should give them plenty of room if they needed it. "That must be nice for everyone."

There was a pause. This was a potentially dicey line of conversation. It hadn't been clear to me when the case wrapped up that the family would be able to navigate some long-standing issues that had surfaced.

Elizabeth came back to the conversation. "Actually, it's quite wonderful having them here. I never had imagined three generations together in this house. I wouldn't have believed how much…happiness has come with the challenges."

Good. That was better than I'd anticipated.

"But you didn't call me to hear an old woman talk about her estrogen-laden household."

"Well, no." Who would? "I hope we might find some time for a brief conversation."

Elizabeth cleared her throat. "That sounds like business."

"Just a bit. It has to do with a reference you provided."

"DeLuna."

"Yes."

"I see. There's just one thing."

"OK."

"I recall we agreed that you should call me Elizabeth."

"We did." Pause. "But I greeted you as Missus Winstrop, didn't I?"

"It's forgivable. I assume you hoped our chat could happen soon?"

"Very soon."

"I'm at home now. Are you nearby?"

"I'm in the village." Everywhere in the village was close to every other where in the village.

"Then I'll get the teapot. You should come here forthwith."

That ended the call. It was a very Elizabeth Winstrop thing to say. I might have preferred to proceed posthaste, but since Elizabeth had asked, I went forthwith instead.

I crossed the street and walked back the way J'Leah and I had come, past Epic Book Shop. Past Asanda Imports, with the courtyard and statues out front and inside the twinkly lights and bling and clothing and jewelry that Cali liked so much. Past Tom's Market where the buskers liked to play. Past the toy store and the hardware store and the bank and the church and the funeral home and into the residential district.

It didn't take long to get from one where in Yellow Springs to another where. In a few minutes I was standing in front of the Winstrop house. An old Honda Civic was parked at the curb, and two somewhat rusty but serviceable-looking bicycles leaned against the porch railing. The gardens and grounds remained immaculate, but there were signs of a more bohemian lifestyle showing. A box fan tucked into an upstairs window. Clothes hanging on a line in the back of the yard. A walking path worn into the grass where someone was cutting from the door to the sidewalk.

I rang the bell. Elizabeth answered with her shoulders back and straight, wearing a casual flowery blouse and an apron. It was the apron that was unusual.

"Jackson."

"Elizabeth."

She nodded at the greeting and gestured me in.

I passed an entry table stacked with books, a handbag, an umbrella. Jackets hung from pegs on the wall beside the door, and a couple pairs of shoes were tucked under the table. That was all new. The inner working of the household had never been visible when it was just Elizabeth here.

She saw me looking. Elizabeth carefully untied the apron and folded it neatly in her hands. "It seems Willow is very partial to fruit pies. I'd forgotten how much I don't mind being in the kitchen."

She led me to the parlor, then departed for the kitchen to deposit the apron and bring out the tea.

I settled into a wingback chair in front of the hearth. Kindling nestled beside the hearth in a basket. Another week or two and there might be enough chill to light a fire. She would be ready.

Elizabeth returned carrying a tray laden with a teapot, cups, and accoutrements. I made to raise, but she nodded me back down and set the tray on a low table centered between the chairs in the room. "So." She lifted a tiny fragile teacup and placed it onto a saucer. "I recall that you took the lavender sugar?"

I had. At Elizabeth's insisting. And it had been palatable but not especially to my liking. I said, "I'll bet that's something your granddaughter would like."

Elizabeth stopped with a cube pinched midair between two tiny tongs. "Actually, Henna really prefers them. It seems she can't get enough."

I put up a palm. "Then why don't you save those for her? I'd be happy with just a touch of milk."

Elizabeth seemed to get my meaning. She lowered the lavender sugar cube back into the bowl and poured two cups of tea with a little milk in each. She held one of those out to me. "And I'll have the same."

She sat, and we sipped. I tried to remember if Brick had taken tea when he'd been here, and I couldn't imagine Brick drinking tea, but I also couldn't imagine anyone not accepting a cup of tea from Elizabeth. Huh.

The aroma of pie hung in the air, but there was no offer of a slice. I assumed the pie was still baking. Maybe if I stayed long enough there would be pastry to go with the tea.

I sipped some more. "I assume Willow is at school?"

Elizabeth nodded. "Home soon."

"She's making friends?"

"She is. She has mentioned your daughter, though I don't know how close they are."

"Well, friends are important."

"They are."

"And Henna?"

Elizabeth set her cup down and straightened it in the saucer. "Henna has taken a job waiting tables. It seems she's done that kind of thing before, though this time she says it's a little different."

I palmed the teacup in my hand, resisting the urge to do the tai chi move and raise the cup. "How so?"

"She appears to like her boss and working there. Which is apparently remarkable for her. It seems that tips are good, and Henna likes the people she works with."

"That's good."

Elizabeth refreshed our tea and added a little more milk, then she sat back between the wings of her chair. It seemed we had given enough time and due diligence to politeness and catching up.

I sat my cup down. "You referred DeLuna to me. I appreciate that. It's good business."

"You're welcome." She lifted her chin. "Though it wasn't…quite like that."

"Oh?"

"I didn't suggest you, quite so much as I just put him in touch with you."

I held a hand out and tilted it back and forth. "Comme ci, comme ça." Like this, like that.

Elizabeth looked surprised by the expression but didn't comment on it. "This new phone. He called and I saw that it was one of… someone who Robert had worked with. My thought was that DeLuna didn't know Robert had passed. But he had heard. He wanted to know who was the detective—private investigator?" She waited for me to respond.

"Either."

She said, "Comme ci, comme ça" and made the motion with her hand. "He wanted the number for the detective who'd found Henna and Willow."

Interesting. That was me, but I wasn't hard to find. Office excluded. DeLuna could have just looked me up. Most mornings I was easy enough to find looking for coffee or breakfast at the Emporium or somewhere in town. Anyway, why call Elizabeth?

She answered that for me. "DeLuna wanted a referral when he contacted you. Someone to say had recommended you."

"I see."

"He seemed to think it was important to…getting your attention, perhaps."

"Hmm?"

"I didn't see the harm."

"No, there's no harm. I appreciate it. There's just been some, uh, unusual things about the work."

Her eyes honed more tightly on me. "This has something to do with the marks on your neck that you're trying to cover?"

I twisted in my chair. "Not cover well enough, I suppose."

Elizabeth let her gaze retreat. "I won't ask further of that. And what of DeLuna has brought you here?"

"Just general diligence. Perhaps if you could just tell me a bit about him. How he knew Robert, or how you knew him. Anything that stands out."

She pulled her shoulders back.

"Without breaching any confidences, of course."

Elizabeth seemed to think for a moment, then she started. "Robert worked with them—both brothers, I suppose, though it was Carlos I mainly knew and interacted with. I recall Carlos was ingenious at something or other, and Robert was very interested in thinking about practical applications. That's the crux of how they planned to work together."

That sounded right.

"We had a few dinners. Robert and I with Carlos and his wife. We may have even hosted them here. I don't recall precisely. It would have been some time ago."

I took out my little notepad and scribbled some lines. Some day I'd move to digital. A notes app, or voice recording. For now, and in the ambiance of Elizabeth's parlor, pen and paper felt right.

"I remember he had a lovely wife, though I can't recall her name right now."

"Judy?"

Elizabeth looked thoughtful. "That seems like it."

"Do you remember anything else about Judy?"

"Like what?"

"Was she healthy?"

"Good lord, is the poor woman sick in some way?"

"Uhm…I didn't mean to—Let me just ask instead if she seemed happy?"

"That seems a rather intimate question."

Oops again. "Apologies."

Elizabeth looked at me and stretched her neck. "I will assume that question has something to do with your work for DeLuna, and that our discussions should be kept as private as possible."

Privacy was something Elizabeth had wanted when I was looking for her daughter, but it hadn't gone that way. The story made the news and gave her much more attention than she'd bargained for. I was sympathetic. I nodded, and Elizabeth continued.

"The wife seemed perfectly happy and content to entertain with me while the men talked business. Or she was good at pretending to be happy about it."

As I supposed that Elizabeth may have also done. I tapped my notepad with the pen. "You're familiar with the DeLunas' work? Or with what they may have worked on or discussed with Robert?"

"I may have known more at one time, but I'm not calling up details now. Something with…electronics? It was more complicated than that."

"Okay." I wrote another quick note.

"The brother, I remember he was interesting."

My pen stopped. "Drummond?"

"Was that his name? I remember it was something unusual."

"Carlos called him Drum."

She raised a finger in recognition. "Yes."

"Unusual how?"

"I only met him once, briefly. It was in Robert's office. He and Carlos were working on something and Drum had joined them. I came in at the end of their meeting, and, heavens, that man could charm a nut from a squirrel if he put his mind to it."

I laughed.

Elizabeth looked surprised.

"I hadn't heard that one. Charm a nut from a squirrel."

"I suppose no one has. My grandmother used to feed peanuts to the squirrels in her yard. That's where it comes from."

I wrote down *nut from a squirrel*. It was something to do. "So Drum was a charmer?"

"He was the salesman, and he was suited to it. Robert and Carlos had some big ideas about him getting them contracts and meeting people."

That fit too with what Carlos had told me.

"The thing I most remember is that they seemed close. And they very much looked like brothers."

I wrote *brothers*. I wouldn't need to go digital if that's all I put in my notes. "Do you know their story? That they came from a small town in Mexico and worked to get educations and come to this country?"

She didn't. We chatted about that for a few minutes. After that I fished for more details, but Elizabeth didn't recall much more about Carlos or Drummond DeLuna.

Finally, she said, "I hope I may have given you something useful."

I scratched my chin. "I don't know. But I thank you." I lifted my teacup and drank. The tea had gone cold, but I finished it anyway and set my cup back into the saucer. "That would be good with pie."

Elizabeth's usually reserved expression broke into a wide grin.

I feigned embarrassment. "I know—shameless. But it smells so good."

"I would never hold it against someone to covet a good piece of pie. But you've come a little too soon. I'd send a slice home with you if it were done."

Ah, Elizabeth Winstrop, such fine use of the subjunctive. I closed my notepad. "I'm sure you would." As we were rising, I turned. "Anything else you might think of, please call me."

She stopped. "One thing."

"OK."

"You could have called. You did, in fact, call. Why come here to ask me about the DeLunas?"

I shrugged. "The tea." And I really liked her.

"You flatter an old woman."

She wasn't so old, but the flattery was real.

We made for the door. Before we reached it, there was the sound of footsteps outside and the door swung wide. Willow Winstrop stepped through. She seemed to recognize me and looked quizzically.

I looked back quizzically. School was out? That meant I was late getting home for Cali, and I had promised not to be.

Elizabeth stepped around me and out onto the porch. "Actually, there is one more thing."

Willow dropped her backpack onto the entry table and disappeared into the house. Following the scent of the pie, probably.

I went outside to join Elizabeth.

"There's a large stone in the garden I'd like to have moved. It's very heavy."

I tried not to blush.

"I believe your friend Mister Brickman may be able to help with it."

"Brick?"

"Yes. With the big muscles."

And what about me? "I'd be happy to give it a try for you. Maybe I can move it."

"I should think your friend would be better suited for it."

Sure he would. "Well point me to it. Let's have a look."

She pointed across the lawn. "There by the entrance to the garden. The stone on the left."

A smile inched up my face. It wasn't such a big stone.

Elizabeth was still pointing. "Do you see? There's a path to the right. If the stone could go on the other side of that path?"

"I think I can do that."

"If you'll just—I have to speak with Willow for just one moment."

I waved a hand. "Sure."

Elizabeth went inside, and I went to the garden. I bent and lifted the stone and carried it across the path. Easy-peasy.

Then I looked around at the squash and pumpkins still on the vines, and a minute or so later Elizabeth came back out. She was looking at something behind the spot where I'd moved the stone from.

I walked over.

Elizabeth pointed to a much larger stone several steps farther into the garden. "It's actually that one I had in mind."

"Oh." I went over and had a look. I bent and wrapped my arms around the granite, straightened my back, and remembered to lift with my legs. The rock came up a few inches. And it immediately went back down again.

I wiped my hands on my pants. "I'll call Brick."

10

I WAS LATE. I walked back downtown to Tom's Market in a hurry.

Tom's is in the heart of the village. For those in town who don't like to keep a lot of things in their cupboards, it's their de facto pantry. And a good one. You drop in, pick up a few things, and head out. It's a small place. Sometimes you can get in and out in a hurry. But sometimes you see someone you know. Then life in a small town kicks in.

It's like talking with your neighbors over the back fence, except it's neighbors from the whole town. It's easy to chat over the produce for a lot longer than you planned to. Today I was in a hurry. I kept my head down.

The woman who sings jazz was out front busking. She was good. I dropped a few dollars into her hat and went inside.

I texted Cali. *Sorry. Running late. Are you at home?*

My phone dinged. *I'm at Tom's.*

Like I said.

Cali texted again. *Went home and you weren't there. We need something for dinner tonight with Marzi.*

I turned down the aisle toward produce and gave a hi-lo whistle. It was the call I used for the cat when I wanted to find her. Cali wasn't the cat, but she knew the call. She turned. "Dad."

She was examining a yellow pepper. I sauntered up. "Got plans for that pepper?"

She set the pepper back into the bin. "No. What are you thinking of making?"

"Tofu."

"Dad."

"I make a really good crispy tofu."

"Sure you do, but Marzi likes meat."

"I know, but I'm cooking. Marzi's happy with vegetarian."

"She's OK with it. I don't know if she's happy."

I held a hand level and wiggled it slightly. "Comme ci, comme ça. I'm working on her."

"Don't do that."

"What?"

"The weird French thing."

"It's not weird if you're French."

"We're not. Can't we at least get something like fish?"

Tough crowd. "Sure. What's like fish?"

"Well, fish."

"OK, let's get fish."

"How about bouillabaisse?"

I almost held back a laugh. "Not that fancy. It's a weeknight. We don't have time." I looked around the produce. Maybe a nice salad. "I don't think we've ever had bouillabaisse. Where'd you pick that up?"

Cali rolled her shoulders. Some kind of a shrug, maybe. "It's just something that we've been wanting to make."

I looked over. "We? You and Marzi?"

It looked like some pink rose in her cheeks. "Me and the girls. We've been making fancy meals."

All right, I was a little surprised. "You've made bouillabaisse?"

"No. That's why I want to try it."

"Good idea. Another night."

"We look up recipes on the internet."

"Uh-huh."

"Mostly Jenny and Asia and me. Jenny likes to cook and we started looking up recipes, and there were these funny videos. And then…" The shoulder roll came again. Whatever.

"Why don't you look up a fish recipe?"

She was already swiping. Looking. Swiping. "Fish tacos?"

I pointed. "Bingo."

She picked up an avocado. "Guacamole."

I lifted a savoy cabbage. "We'll want slaw."

Cali read from her phone. "Carrots, red onion, a lemon." She reached into produce bins. "Got it, got it, getting it."

OK. Sympatico so far. This felt good. I ad-libbed. "Corn chips."

"Of course."

"Salsa." Her fingers worked the phone. "For salsa we'll need tomatoes, a pepper, cilantro."

"We could just buy a jar."

She made a face. "We'll want *good* stuff. Marzi's coming over."

It seemed that Cali was working harder for the date than I was. That should tell me something. I gave in. "Pick up a lime or two with that."

I hoisted up a fat yam and placed it into the basket. I didn't ask. I knew how to roast a good yam with paprika and onion.

Cali and I debated over fish until we decided on trout. I would have picked up the cod, but Cali wanted the good stuff. Then I scanned our basket. "Ready?"

"Wine."

"We have seltzer at home."

She smiled brightly. "Wine?"

"It's a weeknight. I don't know if there'll be much of that."

I got something less flattering than the smile. "Dad, I feel like I'm working harder for this date than you are."

Funny, I was just thinking that. "OK, wine. We'll have to go to the Emporium for that."

Cali swept an arm out. "Lay on, Macduff."

I laughed.

"What?"

"No, it's a good laugh. You actually said that right."

Her eyes rolled. "I've read Shakespeare."

Of course she had. "But it might not mean exactly what you think it does."

She flung her arm as if brandishing an imaginary sword.

"All right. Maybe you do." I laid on. No one noticed the swordplay in the aisle. Typical day at Tom's Market.

We checked out and I looked down the street trying to remember where I'd left the truck.

Cali handed me the bag of groceries. "I rode my bike."

"You want a ride? We can throw the bike in the back."

She kept going. "Why would I want a ride home when I have my bike?"

Yup. That was my daughter.

I carried the groceries to the truck and beat her home by about a minute. It's that kind of town.

I had emptied everything from the bag onto the counter when Cali came in. She picked up the avocado. "I've got the guac."

I rolled a lime her way. "Try not to let it get brown."

She frowned. "I won't let you down."

"*Brown*. Don't let the avocado turn brown."

She giggled.

I gave her a look.

She said, "You sound like Dr. Seuss when you say that."

I repeated it, in a more exaggerated voice. I got another giggle, smaller than the first. I knew when to stop. We went back to the food.

Cali opened a cupboard door and looked at the little bowls and ramekins inside. "We should do *mise en place*."

I stopped mid-slice on the cabbage. "You told me not to do the weird French thing."

"It's not weird when I do it."

"Of course." I resisted the urge to say *d'accord*. "Where did you learn that? And how to pronounce it?"

She tipped a finger toward her phone. "It's a whole big world out there."

And I was enjoying the small world in our kitchen. I went back to making the slaw. "Why don't we do this more often?"

Cali sniffed as she sliced onion. "What? Cook together? Or have Marzi over?"

"I meant cook, but having Marzi over too."

She sliced. "You've been busy."

"We all are through the week. It's a distraction."

The knife came down to the cutting board. "Marzi's distraction is your line of work."

So much for our happy moment. We'd been through this before. I didn't think there was quite as much to that as Cali made out, but now didn't seem the time to protest. Marzi would be here soon. Cali and I could sort this out later when we weren't in front of company.

I mixed onion and carrot into the cabbage and worked on the slaw. "Maybe you should take some classes."

Cali looked confused.

"Cooking classes."

She brightened. "There's some good videos online."

Not quite what I'd meant, but whatever made her happy again.

When everything was ready except putting the fish on the grill, I carried some things to the table. Plates, water glasses, silverware. I made a show of finding the cloth napkins and folding three of them onto the table. On a weeknight. Look at me. I'm being fancy for my date.

Cali followed with her own show of placing the bottle of wine in the center of the table and getting two glasses and a corkscrew from the cupboard. She pretended to wipe away an imaginary spot on the rim of a glass. Well done. So we were having some fun again.

I went out to heat the grill. Once I was alone, a subroutine that had been trying to run through my head resurfaced. CDE. I didn't want to dwell on it, but I wanted to go back to the compound. Just take another look. Maybe I'd take Brick or J'Leah with me.

Bad idea, Jackson. And get your mind back on your daughter and your date. Marzi would be here any minute.

I laid the trout on the grill and forced myself to hum a tune in my head to stop the distracting thoughts. I found myself whistling Mull of Kintyre, the bagpipe bit near the end. That did it.

I brought the fish in. Marzi arrived and Cali met her at the door, hung her jacket, and led her to the kitchen where a tray with salsa, guac, chips, and olives waited.

Marzi sat on a high stool at the counter, looked at the spread, and said, "Very nice, after the day I've had." She delicately picked up a chip and tried the guacamole. She smiled, said, "Lovely."

Cali blushed. I pointed to her. "New chef in town."

Marzi took another chip and tried the salsa. "Excellent. So fresh."

Cali eyed me. "See? I told you."

She had.

We opened the wine, and it was starting to be a good night. The food was good, and the company took care of itself. The wine may have helped. I don't know why I felt a little relieved when we were cleaning up.

Then Marzi noticed something. She stood to get a closer look as I loaded dishes into the sink. "Jackson, what happened to your neck?"

Cali answered before I got a word out. "It's not just his neck. You should see his back and legs."

I gave Cali a look. You're not helping.

Marzi lifted my collar and looked.

Cali said, "He got cut up at work."

I pulled away and stopped with the dishes. "It's not what—Look, that makes it sound worse than it was. I just got tangled in some fencing."

Marzi's eyes roamed over me like she was looking for other marks. "At work?"

I wiped my hands on a towel. "Long story."

Cali said, "And he won't tell it."

I shook my head. Lord, if I'd mentioned the guards and the gunshot. "What's the big deal about a few scratches?"

Cali rolled her eyes. "That's why Marzi doesn't come over more often. She doesn't like you getting hurt at work."

"Cali." I tossed the towel on the counter. "Marzi is right here. She can speak for herself. And this is something for her and I to talk about. Not you."

The spell was officially broken.

Cali rolled her eyes to Marzi.

Marzi's role here was complicated. She'd been our therapist when we lost Kat. She knew our secrets and our history. But now she wasn't our therapist. Now she was someone I wanted to date and someone Cali wanted to move in with us right now, tonight, and fill the void where her mother was missing. Patience didn't seem to fit with Cali's sense of teenage drama.

Marzi turned carefully to Cali. "I think maybe we're all involved. But it is something your dad and I should talk about. Our relationship is larger than this one thing. We're still finding our way. It takes time."

Cali didn't look convinced.

"I trust your father when he says he's careful in his work."

Now I felt really guilty about the gunshot.

"And I know that his job has some risks, which I believe your father can navigate."

Cali's frown softened. "Does that mean you're going to stay the night?"

Marzi retreated. "Uhm…"

I stepped forward. "That's a question for Marzi and I to decide."

Marzi spoke softly but firmly. "Probably not tonight. But that doesn't mean we aren't…"

I don't know what word Marzi was searching for. Before she could find it, Cali stormed off. "If you're not staying, then what's the point?"

There were heavy footsteps and then Cali's door closed.

I held my hands out in surrender. "Sorry. She misses her mother. It's not fair that she expects you to fill that void."

Marzi had a strange look on her face. Then she finished her previous thought. "It doesn't mean that I'm not interested." She took me by the hand and walked me out onto the porch. A chill was teasing but hadn't fully set in yet.

We sat in two of the chairs and faced each other. I said, "If you have any advice, I'd appreciate it."

Marzi took both of my hands in hers. "I'm not your therapist. I was, and that complicates things. It brings an already established sense of closeness and trust between Cali and me that wouldn't normally have developed yet. That's part of why she's responding the way she is."

My hands twitched under Marzi's. "It seems like she's pressuring me to…you know. Have a sleepover. And right when I'm worried about her starting to think the same thing about boys."

Marzi nodded. "She wants me to stay, and what that implies, because she sees it as a sign of a committed relationship."

"Well that's ironic, don't you think? Given Cali's age and what the boys around her are probably thinking? I don't think one night means..." I stopped. Bad idea, Jackson.

Marzi put her eyes on mine. "I said I wasn't going to be your therapist. And I'm not. *You*—" she pointed— "have a difficult parenting situation. And *me*—" she pointed again— "I'm implicit in that to some extent. But I'm also on a date right now. And I don't think it's over yet?"

It was a question. I wished right then I had a slice of that pie from Elizabeth Winstrop. Something simple to do. Put on some decaf, click forks, eat a little pie. Normal. Easy. No sweat. No pressure. Cali might even come back out for pie.

But then Marzi took my hand and led us back inside. It turned out she had something in mind too. And we didn't need the pie.

11

AS PROMISED, Marzi didn't stay the night. Other than the downside of an empty bed, after she left the thoughts I'd been pushing away had no more distraction and crawled back into my head.

The first thing I did in the morning was text J'Leah. I asked if she had any news yet, and I told her I planned to go out and take another look at the CDE compound.

Her response was clipped: *IN.*

Hmm.

She followed up. *Nothing on my end. I'm going to CDE with you.*

Good. I hadn't even asked her yet.

We agreed to take her car. It was a vehicle no one at the compound had seen before. We hashed out a few details and left the rest to figure out on the way.

I made coffee and a breakfast sandwich of leftovers. Cali roused herself and stayed in the bathroom for a long time with the shower running. She came to the kitchen dressed and with watery eyes and poured a splash of coffee.

I refilled my own cup. "Good morning."

She looked at the table. "What's this?"

"Sandwich."

She lifted the top. "What's on it?"

"Leftovers."

"Are those the sweet potatoes?"

"They are."

She pressed the top back down, lifted the sandwich, and took a bite. It must have gone down all right. She wrapped the rest of the sandwich in her napkin. "I'm taking this with me."

"OK."

Then she picked up her backpack and jacket and walked out the door. No comments about the night before. Like nothing untoward had happened. I chose to take that as a sign of progress.

I packed binoculars, a water bottle, and some other items into a backpack and went out onto the porch to wait for J'Leah. A few minutes later, an all-electric, slate-gray Chevy Bolt pulled in front of the house.

I walked over and bent to look inside. The passenger window came down. J'Leah was in the driver's seat. Her eyes roamed past me and over the house. "Nice place, Jackson."

"Nice car. What happened to the Honda?"

"Nothing. Honda's great. I sold it and bought this instead."

"You'll get better gas mileage."

"Good one. But my electric bill will go up."

"Price you pay for being climate-sensitive."

"I think the word you're looking for is climate-centric."

"Climate-centric? Is that what they're calling it now?"

"It's one of the things. Depends on who you talk to. The car needs electricity, and it has heavy metals in the batteries and there's a manufacturing and recycling toll."

"So it's not all good?"

"Few things are. But it's better than my old car."

It was. "Would you rather a jet pack?"

"Depends what it would run on."

"We could bicycle out. Runs on people power."

"You wouldn't be able to keep up with me. Are you going to get in?"

My hand lingered on the door handle. "Will we want two vehicles? I can follow you in the truck."

She shook her head. "You're going to wait in the bushes. Get in."

So she'd been thinking about the details. And it looked like she was giving me the unglamorous job. I guessed I deserved it. I got in.

J'Leah's plan was simple. She would drop me close enough to the CDE compound to watch through the binoculars. She'd drive to the entry gate and ask to see Carlos. Say she was working a private job for him. That was true enough, but none of the guards or others had met her. We expected that she'd be turned away, the same reception I'd gotten at my first approach. When that happened, J'Leah would announce that she was calling Carlos to clear things up. Instead she would call me, and I would explain to whoever was working the gate that I was the guy Carlos had hired for the security check. That should set off bells. The reaction might tell us if Carlos had ever briefed his team, or if they were left to believe it had been a real break-in.

I would press the matter with Carlos depending on how that went. It wasn't rocket science. And it might not gain us much. But we didn't need rocket science, and sometimes a little push is enough to topple over something larger. I'd be happy just to have a look around in the daylight without anyone shooting at me.

Once that was settled, I relaxed in my seat. The little electric car hummed quietly down the narrow back road. I tried the electric windows, the electric seat. Nice. I looked over at J'Leah. "So it's all electric. Is it fast?"

She punched the pedal. The little car shot forward.

"OK, so it's fast. You Millennials know how to spend your money."

She slowed to a reasonable speed. "Yeah. Avocado toast and shave clubs."

"Shave clubs?"

"You don't know what a shave club is?"

"No. A bunch of hairy people getting together to shave? Once a week kind of thing? Sounds like my kind of party."

She looked at me like she wanted to know if I was kidding. "It's a subscription."

"Like Netflix?"

"But without the movies."

"So it's a subscription to shaving?"

"Razors and things."

"Wait, it comes in the mail? Like a record club?"

"Yeah, but not by Pony Express, like your record clubs did."

"OK, so the razors and things come every day? Isn't that a lot?"

"No. That would be ridiculous. It's like once a month."

"So you just shave once a month?"

"No. Are you really—" And then she probably realized that I was trying to push her buttons.

"What if I don't use everything before the month is up and the next batch of things arrives? Say I still have some razors and shaving cream left. After a few months, that could be a lot of shaving cream."

She sighed heavily. "I don't know. Shave more often?"

"Mmm. And would I use up the other things? What sorts of other things would be involved?"

"Well, razors. But like, shave butter and stuff."

"Shave butter?"

"And shave dew. You put it on after."

"Shave dew?"

"I'm not making that up."

"It sounds like you are. What about somebody who doesn't have much to shave? Like a guy who has a beard and just shaves around the edges, like on his neck, compared to a woman who shaves her legs? That's a lot more surface area."

J'Leah let another heavy sigh. "Why are we talking about this?"

"You brought it up?"

"I did?"

"Avocado toast and shave clubs."

"I didn't mean for me. Like, other people."

"Would you rather talk about avocado toast?"

"No."

"You sure? I think it might help explain some things about our youngest generations."

She didn't argue. Instead, J'Leah said, "Maybe so. But your generation—*generations*—screwed things up for us. If the world doesn't last, it won't be the worst thing if we go out clean-shaven."

I thought about it. "Maybe so."

We rode the rest of the way in silence, just the hum of the car and the whirr of tires against the blacktop. It really was quite nice.

When the CDE compound was almost in view, I held a hand up. "Hang on. Cameras."

J'Leah slowed.

"I didn't mark them, but from what Carlos said there's at least one at the road."

She raised her foot from the pedal. The car was in one-pedal mode and it decelerated and braked and drove a charge back into the battery. Cool. The car almost stopped. J'Leah said, "How far?"

"You'll see it on the left. Maybe a quarter mile away around that curve."

She drifted to the berm. "Then this is your stop."

I picked up my backpack and pulled on a ball cap.

The Bolt stopped and J'Leah pulled her visor down against the sun. "Can you pick a spot?"

I squinted, then pointed to the side of the road opposite the compound. "Behind that honeysuckle. Corn behind it hides the house. I'll walk the edge of the corn behind the honeysuckle."

"Good. Think you can get right across from the entry?"

"I think so."

She looked at her phone in the dash holder. "Four minutes."

I'd have to hustle. "I'll ping you when I'm there."

And I was out. I ducked under the honeysuckle, jutted left, and jogged along the rows of corn. Three-and-a-half minutes later I texted J'Leah.

A few seconds after that, the little gray Bolt came into view down the road. I raised the binoculars and settled on a view of the guard shack at the entry gate.

The sky was clear and the compound was brightly lit under the sun. Ten or so cars were parked in the gravel lot just inside the fence. They were mostly late-model and at least mid-luxury range. The CDE employees seemed to be doing well.

More cars were parked farther back inside the fence around another building, and I noticed now some picnic tables under a metal awning that would make a nice outdoor lunch spot.

The Bolt slowed and made an almost soundless turn onto the farm-house drive. When J'Leah reached the gate, I glassed her head extending from the window and saw her speaking into the video camera, just as I'd done.

A moment later a man in dark blue trousers and a light blue polo shirt emerged from the building where the interior security office was located. He wasn't wearing the uniform that the three guards from two nights before had been dressed in.

The tall chain-link gate in front of J'Leah rolled back as the man walked through. He crossed in front of the Bolt and came directly to the window where J'Leah leaned out.

They chatted for a moment. It looked like a pleasant exchange. Then the guard pointed into the compound toward the farmhouse where I'd encountered the trouble.

The guard made a call on his cell phone and nodded while he listened. He ended the call and waved J'Leah in.

Hmm. Carlos DeLuna seemed to be on the premises.

J'Leah parked with the other cars in the gravel lot. The big entry gate rolled closed, and the guard walked with J'Leah to the farmhouse. She and the guard waited a moment, then Carlos came out, held a hand up against the sun in his eyes, and offered the other palm for J'Leah to shake.

Huh.

Then J'Leah and Carlos walked. He guided her to one of the picnic tables beneath the awning and they sat. Then they talked. About what, I didn't know.

Twelve minutes later, J'Leah and Carlos stood. He walked with her to the Bolt. She got in and he waved as she navigated back toward the open gate.

I tucked the binoculars back into my pack, turned back down the row of corn, and kicked up my knees and ran.

I emerged approximately where I thought J'Leah had let me out into the brush. When I pushed through the honeysuckle, she had the little car on the edge of the road twenty feet in front of me. Not bad.

I got in and J'Leah pressed her foot and the Bolt started silently moving. Not exactly bolting away. I kept that thought to myself.

I stashed the backpack at my feet. "Well, that looked cozy."

J'Leah looked over. "You know, it kind of was. The man never met me before, and he acted like we were old friends."

"He does that."

She drove.

I opened a water bottle and drank. "And your cover is blown. I assume you told him your name and said you were the specialist working with me?"

"He didn't ask my name."

"Odd."

She agreed. "He didn't seem to care."

"Well, he does just seem to want to get rid of us."

"That was my feeling."

I brought up another thing. "That guard was wearing a different uniform from the three the other night when I was here."

"Also odd."

"And he seemed a lot nicer."

"Said his name was John. Tried to chat me up a little."

"Looked like it."

"Kind of cute. Maybe he'll be that nice boy you said I should settle down with."

I figured she was joking. I didn't make any effort to confirm that. "What did you and Carlos talk about?"

"I had to make up some stuff. Asked about back-up servers, remote access, redundancy. Sort of caught me off guard that he was there and I got in to talk to him."

"Is any of what you talked about important for the cyber check?"

"Not really."

"You think that tipped him off?"

"To what?"

"Anything?"

She maneuvered through a sharp curve. The car hugged the road like it was on rails. "Doubt it. He talked a lot, but he didn't really say much of anything."

"He should have wondered why you drove out to talk with him. Especially without notice. You could have called or emailed, or asked me to put you two together."

"He didn't seem to even think about that. Just came out and we started talking."

"Did you tell the guard you were there about the security check?"

"John."

"OK. Did you tell John, the cute guy you might think about settling down with, that you were there about a security check?"

"No."

"So we still don't really know if the security folks there have been fully briefed, or briefed at all, by Carlos."

"Or by anyone else."

I scratched my chin. "What do you mean?"

"Carlos could have asked someone else to brief the security team. He didn't necessarily have to do that himself."

I turned it over. "Why does that matter?"

"I don't know if it does. I thought we were just riffing here."

I let out a breath. "We are. That didn't even seem like the same place I went to the other night."

"It doesn't seem like what you described. It's too soft. Almost like it's for show."

I thought back to my meeting with Carlos the day before. "Maybe some of it was."

We didn't seem to be getting anywhere, and I thought the trip out here hadn't been worth the time or gas. Well, worth the time or electrons. At least the drive was nice. Corn and soy turning early-autumn brown and gold.

Then J'Leah said, "Carlos said to say hi to you."

I rubbed my temples. "Something doesn't fit here."

"He just wants the report. Said if we finished early, that would be his preference."

I'll bet it would. He'd said the same to me. But what happened to the security team? Where had everyone gone?

12

FEELING MANLY?

That was code for a workout. I texted Brick back. *Got a special warmup for you.*

He sent back, *Pick you up in ten.* He didn't ask what the warmup was.

I let Elizabeth Winstrop know that we were coming over to move her rock.

She replied. *I just took a pie out of the oven. Maybe Mr. Brickman would like a slice.*

I was pretty sure she knew his name was Brick, not Mr. Brickman. And now I was also pretty sure he was her favorite.

Brick rolled up in the Shelby and we rumbled across the village to the curb in front of Elizabeth's. I skipped the door and we went straight to the garden and I showed Brick the little rock I'd moved by myself.

He laughed loud. "Little baby rock. Haven't I been working you hard enough? Gonna have to move you down to the little pink weights."

"My bad." I pointed. "It's that one."

Brick's eyes went to the bigger rock. "Oh."

"I could move it on my own, but Elizabeth wants you. I think she's sweet on you."

"Who is sweet on whom?" It was Elizabeth's voice from behind us. Willow had come out with her.

"I was just telling Brick that—"

"I heard what you said. And you most certainly were unable to move that rock by yourself."

Brick laughed again. Then he cleared his throat and said, "Mrs. Winstrop."

She frowned. "Elizabeth, I believe."

"Elizabeth."

She gestured to Willow. "You remember my granddaughter?"

"I do." Brick offered his hand. It's not something I would have done, but Willow didn't hesitate to take Brick's hand and shake. There was one pump, then they broke the clasp. Brick said, "Willow. Quando said he knows you from around town."

"Quando?"

Brick put a hand about chin height. "Yay tall, big shoulders." He dropped the hand. "Wears shirts that hang down past his—"

"I know him."

"OK." Brick looked at the girl. "Anyway, he knows you. I'm sure he'd want me to tell you he said hi."

Willow looked pinched.

Brick looked to me and Elizabeth as if for guidance. I didn't have any to offer.

The look on Willow's face passed. "You're his dad?"

Now Brick looked pinched, or like he'd been stepped on. "No, I'm um…" He cleared his throat. "Quando is, uh…"

"Oh."

"I just mean that…"

Willow raised her hands. "No, it's OK."

Brick looked relieved that the conversation was over.

But it wasn't. Willow said, "I've seen him at the…skate park and stuff. He said he's living at this really cool place outside of town."

Brick looked as surprised to hear Quando had said that as I was.

Willow said, "But I haven't, you know, seen him around school?" It was a question.

Brick didn't answer.

Willow tried again. "Maybe he goes somewhere else?"

It got quiet. And awkward. What we had here was a runaway, whose mother had run away, talking to a strange man who had taken in a runaway, in front of Elizabeth, who until recently had seemed perfectly content that her daughter had run away. And Brick was hiding that he didn't know what to do about Quando, who was a runaway.

Willow shied. "Never mind. Just tell him I said hi."

She left us and walked back toward the house. I thought there might be a little more in it than Willow had let on. Maybe the new guy in town was getting some attention. But I let it go. None of my business.

Elizabeth watched Willow retreat into the house. It was such a change from the solitary and private woman I'd met a few months before.

Brick turned to Elizabeth and broke the spell. "I hear you've got a little job that's a bit too much for Jackson."

I hung my head. "I'm right here. I can hear you." I went to the rock and bent and wrapped my arms around it. "Y'all keep talking. I'll just do this myself."

Brick came over and bent down. "Don't hurt yourself."

"Haven't yet."

"You wish that were true. Lift."

We did. The rock came up an inch, moved sideways four or five inches, and came back down hard.

I looked over the granite at Brick. "Count your toes."

"Still got five."

"Sounds bad. You should have ten."

"Har-har. Haven't ever got hurt yet. Lift."

We did, and eventually the rock inched to where it made Elizabeth happy. She said, "You know, watching you two makes me remember something my late husband Robert used to say. Don't lift it if you can drag it, don't drag it if you can roll it, and don't roll it if you can leave it there."

I looked at the rock. "You mean we could have just left it where it was?"

"No." Elizabeth waved toward the house. "Now that's done, I hope you have time for tea?"

They both heard me laugh. Here was my chance. See Brick drinking lavender tea from a dainty little cup, his finger held out as he sipped.

Brick clasped Elizabeth's hand. "Nice as that sounds, we have to get going."

"Then you'll take a slice of pie with you? Apple-plum, straight from the oven."

Apple-plum? That sounded amazing.

Brick said, "If you don't mind, I might take a slice home to the boy."

Elizabeth turned for the house. "Excellent. And one for you?"

"I lean away from sweets." Brick touched his abs. They were probably as hard as the rock we'd just moved.

Elizabeth started walking. "Maybe this will be a special occasion for you. Did I say it's apple-plum?" It didn't sound like a question. So two slices for Brick.

When we reached the door, Elizabeth held it open and said, "Jackson, perhaps you'd like a slice too?"

"Now that you mention it." I followed Brick inside, thinking how I'd divide that slice between me and Cali. Half and half? Two-thirds and one-third? Did Cali have to know there'd been pie?

When we were back in the Shelby with our still-warm apple-plum pie, I peeked inside the paper bag Elizabeth had wrapped the slices in.

Brick started the car. "That's for later."

"Says who? We're not really going to work out now, are we? When there's pie."

The Shelby rumbled. "That's how you're in the shape you're in now."

I patted my stomach. "I do my best."

"Tell you what. I'll carry Betty around the yard. You can watch me and eat pie. Then we'll see who can move the biggest rock."

I folded the top of the bag back down and put the pie away. It only hurt a little.

I was starting to relax. Letting the DeLuna thing drift out of my head, thinking about what would come along next. There was a clear blue sky overhead, I was riding in a vintage sports car, Billie Joel was playing on the radio, and there was pie. What was there not to be happy about?

A shiny green Chevelle answered that question. It came in hot behind the Shelby when Brick slowed for a turn. Brick turned right, and the Chevelle came around beside and made the turn with us, right off Brick's door, the Chevelle screaming and skidding and digging for the road. We popped out of the turn and the Chevelle jumped ahead and took the lane in front of us.

Brick slowed. "Friend of yours?"

"No."

"You expecting trouble?"

"No." But gears started turning. Something with DeLuna I hadn't anticipated? I touched my belt where I'd carried my pistol as a deputy, remembered it wasn't there. "You packing?"

"Beneath the seat."

The Chevelle slowed. Brick slowed behind it. "Sometimes people see the car, they want to play."

"Yeah, but a Chevelle?"

Brick slowed some more. "I do not want to scratch this car."

The Chevelle drifted onto the center line and stopped. There were no other cars on the stretch of road, just a long curve ahead and a few houses set back from the route.

Brick stopped, his eyes on the Chevelle and the driver in it, his hand on the gear shift. "What do you think?"

I felt something heating up inside me. I tried to tamp it down. "Doesn't look right."

Brick pushed the shift into reverse. A big guy came out of the Chevelle. He carried something in one hand that looked like a sawed-off baseball bat.

Brick eased the clutch and the Shelby inched backward. "Any reason to stay?"

"Nope."

Then the guy stopped walking. The bat came down. He yelled. "You're not those kids."

Brick stopped. "What'd he say?"

The man turned back to the Chevelle. I was confused. But Brick didn't seem to be. He jumped out, ran three steps, and grabbed the guy by the elbow and spun him around. The bat came up again but Brick blocked it and sent the lumber clattering onto the road.

The big guy's hat flew off. "Man, let me go. Get off me." He rolled his shoulders and tried to pull his arms away from Brick.

I was out of the car now and watched Brick wrap the guy up and bend him over the bumper of the Chevelle. I called out. "Let's go."

Brick wasn't having it. He pushed the guy's head down to the bumper. "What was all that?"

"Let go. I thought you was them kids."

Brick softened his grip a little.

The guy grunted. "They's some kids drive up and down here. They speed. I thought you was them."

Brick let go now.

"I got a little girl in my yard. It ain't safe the way they drive."

I reached Brick and touched his arm. "Come on."

Brick pointed a finger at the man. "You—" His head twitched like a bulldog ready to jump. "You think—"

I pulled Brick's arm.

He came with me, but backward, shouting at the man. "You think driving like that is going to keep your daughter safe, you're a fool."

"Yes, sir." The man's head went down.

"And a Chevelle's got no business messing with a Shelby."

I pushed Brick around the Shelby and got in the passenger door. Brick followed but he fumed.

The big man was back in his car and making a three-point turn. He drove past us the other way without looking over.

A school bus appeared on the curve ahead and motored toward us. I clicked my seat belt. "Let's go."

"Stupid…"

"Let's go."

Brick did. "Lot of trouble for nothing."

We passed the bus and were on open road again. I looked back at the kids' profiles in the windows. "Guy had a point, I guess."

Brick didn't seem to agree. He shifted up a gear. "What is wrong with people?"

"Lots of things."

And there went our good mood. Just that fast. One moment we were in a Shelby on the back roads, happy as larks, pie in the back seat, and the next moment it was spoiled. I tried to get some levity back. "Better not have messed up my pie."

"Pie's fine."

I tried another angle. "Chevelle's not fast enough for a Shelby?"

That got a reaction. Brick grunted. "Not cool enough to mess with a Shelby."

Oh, good. Maybe the mood could be salvaged.

It was a drive to Brick's place, and when we got there I was ready for a workout to burn off what was left of the dark cloud. We stepped up to Betty and I took my jacket off.

Betty is a 1978 Buick Skylark, or parts of a Skylark, that Brick has arranged in the yard. They're staged to kind of look like the car, only there's just an engine block, the chassis, some rims, and other heavy parts sitting in the grass and weeds.

We carry the parts around the cabin, and sometimes out around the yard, and bring them back and rearrange them into the ghost of the Skylark again. Brick has devised all sorts of carries and variations to make the workout as painful as possible.

When we get done with that, he moves us to a complicated climb up thin rails of lumber screwed to the side of the barn. Some of it involves leaps and hanging by a few fingers.

I don't think that's how they trained in the Marines. But Brick was stronger than any Marine I'd ever met.

Brick carried his pie into the cabin. I waited outside and stretched some muscles.

When Brick came back out, his eyes roamed the yard. "You seen Quando?"

"No. Should I?"

"He's not inside."

"Maybe he's at the skate park."

Brick had a strange look. "Maybe. Long walk to town."

"How's he usually get there?"

"Don't know. I've picked him up a few times. I don't know how he gets there."

"Worried about it?"

His brow wrinkled. "Not too much, I guess."

"Probably making friends, he's getting a ride."

"Be nice. Be nice if I knew where he was."

Brick was sounding very fatherly. I didn't say that. We bent to the engine block. Just before we lifted, my phone chirped.

I stopped and looked at the screen. Carlos DeLuna. I accepted the call. "Carlos."

"You're fired."

"Uh—"

"I won't be needing your services anymore."

"Hang on. What's got you in a twist?"

"No twist. We're just done."

"But I—"

"Listen, Jackson. Just take your money and go. We're done." He ended the call.

I stared at the phone. I wanted to do just as Carlos said and let it go. But the missing pieces bothered me. And just like that, the black cloud was back again.

13

WE CARRIED THE ENGINE PARTS around the yard. Crab-walked the engine block around the cabin, turned, switched sides, and crab-walked it back.

I was steamed about the call from DeLuna and pressing harder than usual. When we set the block back into place on its pallet and timbers, I sat and breathed.

Brick stayed on his feet. "What are you doing?"

"Resting."

"Resting is for the weak."

"And those who eat pie. That's how I got in the shape I'm in."

The cloud was lifting. One trip with Betty and I was letting go. See how easy?

I rolled a shoulder in a circle, rubbed the joint, and stood up. "No pain, no pain."

We carried the block again, then the chassis in a complicated carry that Brick had designed to torture a different set of muscles. Then we raced around the cabin carrying the rims.

I was wiping sweat with my shirt and breathing hard when Brick started for the barn. The next set of torture.

We skipped the fingertip climbs on the outside of the barn and went straight inside to the bench and the free weights.

That's where he really made me look silly. We worked hard for almost an hour. When I could barely lift my arms over my head, I cried uncle.

Just to show his superiority, Brick did another set on the bench while I sat and drank water.

He pointed to a row of cabinets over a long wooden workbench. "Apples and walnuts in there."

"Halfway to a pie."

"Better than pie."

"Don't let Elizabeth hear you say that."

He continued his last show-off set, and I indulged in the apples and nuts.

And then it hit me. I took out my phone. "I've got to call J'Leah."

Brick grunted under the weights. "She probably won't answer. You should text."

I stepped out of the barn into the sun and texted. *Full Stop. Was it something you did?*

My phone rang right away. J'Leah said, "What?"

"Full stop."

"Something I did?"

"I'm asking. Carlos just fired us. Wondering if you got somewhere and that spooked him."

"Why would he fire us now, after the weird way he handled it already?"

"That's what I'm wondering. You find anything?"

"I did, but they don't know it."

"You're sure?"

She didn't answer.

"Tell me what you got."

"I had a look around. Got in more than one place. Copied a few things to prove I'd done it."

"That could be what spooked him."

"It doesn't make sense. It's what he asked you to do."

"None of this has made a lot of sense." I took a breath. "We can just forget the whole thing. Right now. Full stop."

"What about the release? If we're fired, does that mean it's not valid anymore? If I break in again, we could be vulnerable?"

"I think we should assume that's what it means."

"OK." There was the sound of typing. "What about the things I already copied? Do we have to return them?"

"I don't know. If they don't know we have anything, it might be a moot question."

"A moot question?"

"It's like a moot point, but it's a question."

"And you think my generation is complicated. So we're not going to tell Carlos I got into their network?"

"I don't think we're going to tell him anything."

"So what do we do with it then?"

It was a good question. "What kind of stuff is there?"

"Photos, video. Some data sheets and spreadsheets. Maybe some kind of budget stuff. Things like that."

"How did you get all that?"

"It's a lot, but it's not a lot. I mean, there's enough to keep you busy looking through it. But compared to what I could have gotten, it's not that much. I just snooped around the edges."

"We should probably delete it?"

"That sounds like a question. We'll have to do more than just delete it if we want it to really be gone. Use a shredder. That will take more work."

We got a big paycheck. We could put in a little time to cover our tracks. "That's probably what we should do."

"Yeah."

"But they probably don't know you got anything."

"Yeah."

"So they wouldn't know if we looked through it."

"Yeah."

"But we're not really on a case, so there's no reason to look through it."

"Yeah. Except, Jackson? Why did Carlos fire you just now?"

"It's weird timing."

"You may want leverage if this isn't over."

"We're both trying to talk ourselves into keeping the files."

"We already have."

We had. "So it probably wouldn't hurt just to take a look at them."

"In case there's something you should know."

"And not because we're snoops."

"Well, technically you are. That's kind of your job."

"J'Leah?"

"Yeah?"

"Why are we still talking about this?"

"Eh…"

"Can you keep the files in a safe place? Somewhere that would be hard to find if someone was looking for them?"

"You mean like if somebody got a warrant?"

"That's what I mean."

"I can do that."

"I don't want you to take on any risk you don't feel comfortable with."

She knew what I meant. "Then let's do this smart. We won't want any digital signatures."

"What does that mean?"

"I'll explain when you get here."

"There?"

"I have a Faraday cage. And no one else will be here until morning." She ended the call and sent me an address.

I texted Cali that I would be late again.

She buzzed me back. *Can I go to Marzi's for dinner?*

Have you asked her?

Is it OK if she says yes?

Sure.

I stepped back into the barn. Brick was sitting on the weight bench eating an apple. I waved. "I notice you can still lift your arms. Maybe you didn't lift enough."

"Har-har." He made a big Popeye muscle on the arm holding the apple.

My phone chirped. Text from Marzi. *I'll feed Cali tonight. I hope you'll be there to join us.*

I hoped so too. I called up the location J'Leah had sent. It was out near the Air Force base. Of course. Very near Carlos' office.

Wright-Patterson Air Force Base is where the Wright Brothers learned to fly, in what was once a marshy meadow north of Dayton. That small flying field among the rattlesnakes and prairie grasses had expanded into an operation that stretched up the valley and lowlands that drain into the Mad River watershed. The base touches on the surrounding cities of Fairborn, Riverside, Beavercreek, and Huber Heights. The National Museum of the United States Air Force sits on the base. So it's big business.

That business drives tech, aviation, and research companies that create civilian jobs that support the base operations. Up and down the highway and roads along the base are strips of buildings that have mysterious names and a lot of people working jobs that wouldn't be there if it wasn't for the military. I was headed for one of those buildings.

I have a cousin who was married to a guy years ago who spent a hitch in the Air Force when he got out of high school. He got stationed at Wright-Patterson and he told a story where he had a grunt job there on a dirt road that disappeared into the woods. He sat in a truck all day with a rifle and handgun and another guy, and they made sure no one went down that road. If anyone tried to pass, they were supposed to shoot them. If one of them went down the road, the other guy in the truck was supposed to shoot him.

He said he didn't know what was down that road in the woods or how long it had been there. But he'd heard stories that they'd sunk entire planes into ponds and lakes in the wetlands there, burying the aircraft and whatever might have been in them down in the mud.

I don't know if my cousin's husband was just telling a good story after a few beers, but I did know the stories about Hangar 18 on the base and the aliens from Roswell who were supposed to have been taken there. Maybe the aliens were at the bottom of one of those ponds. I hoped not.

There was a gate entry to the lot J'Leah sent me to. More security than at Carlos' building. I texted J'Leah and she sent a one-time code and the gate went up automatically and let me in. Not too tough so far, if you knew someone on the inside. Then she met me at the door and I scanned my driver's license into an electronic monitoring system in the vestibule, got approved, and we were in. Not hard to access, but they'd know I'd been there if anyone cared to look. If it didn't bother J'Leah, it didn't bother me.

She led me down a set of stairs into a basement hallway and a room at the far end. Inside was the view I'd seen on our video call when we listened to the trombone caroler out the window. It was a fairly large room with cinderblock walls and several empty desks stacked with computers and monitors and other equipment and scattered notes and files. It was all open office space.

I looked around. "Very progressive. No cubicles to separate everyone and establish hierarchy."

J'Leah rolled her eyes. "There's that, and you can also get distracted all day by everyone on their phones and computers and crunching loud snacks."

"So there are drawbacks."

"If I never have to watch Ted eat another Rice Krispies treat one single crispy at a time, that would be a plus."

She took me to a desk against the back wall. I assumed it was her desk, or some shared-space progressive thing. The Faraday cage was next to it. The cage was a large box made of an open mesh grid of metal. I could see right through. Inside was a small desk and a couple of chairs and not much room for anything else. About the size of my office if it was a screened-in room.

I knew generally how the cage worked. It was like the metal mesh on a microwave door that blocked the longer microwave signals from getting through and kept them only inside the little oven. But a Faraday cage will block nearly all electromagnetic waves—radio, cell phones, Wi-Fi, Bluetooth, and near field communication like credit card taps. Nothing gets in or goes out.

J'Leah opened the door to the Faraday cage. "You know how this works?"

"Like a microwave oven."

She laughed suspiciously. "Sometimes it does feel like I'm getting cooked in there. If you're going to bring your phone in, turn it off. It can transmit to other devices inside the cage."

I turned my phone off. "Isn't this a bit of overkill?"

"It is." We went inside. "A lot of what I do in my work is overly cautious. I guess it's become habit."

"That's what makes you the professional."

She sat at the little desk. I took one of the chairs and scooted around next to her as best I could in the small space. J'Leah reached back to shut the metal door and latch it. "We're going to move and store files that don't belong to us. CDE contracts with government agencies. There are a lot of things that can be embedded into digital files, including code to execute commands like initiating an RF signal. That could leave a digital trace and location reveal if someone was looking for it. They probably won't be, but these are protocols for my work in a situation like this."

I was suitably impressed. And J'Leah got to it.

She showed me CDE spec sheets for circuitry and hardware and purchase prices for parts. That looked like budget stuff, but someone with a better knowledge of electrical or computer engineering could probably glean what the pieces might be used for. We looked quickly through those items.

There were some communication records, emails and such. None of that looked like anything we could make something of.

After about forty-five minutes, J'Leah leaned away from the laptop screen. "Is there something particular we're looking for?"

"That would make it easier, wouldn't it? But I think we're just being nosy. Maybe we should just move the files over and put them away. There probably won't ever be a reason to need them."

She closed some windows and opened a new folder. "Pictures might be worth a few minutes. Since we're just snooping."

I got the feeling she'd already had a preview. "Right. Just for fun."

We skimmed through some boring stuff. Staged photos of people shaking hands. Old pictures of the farm buildings before the fences went up and the improvements were made. Drone shots looking down on the compound. I'd seen that before.

We looked for a lot more than a few minutes. Then I leaned back from the screen. "It's not very interesting."

"I don't think we expected it to be. Lots of these are just still shots from video."

That made me remember the cameras. "There's video?"

"Loads of it." J'Leah tapped the keyboard, and lists of video records showed on the screen.

I looked over her shoulder. "Do you have anything from the surveillance cameras?"

She tapped some more. "Looks like it."

"The gate? Out by the road?"

We both squinted to try to make sense of the naming conventions—how the files were named so someone would know what they were. J'Leah picked up on something that made sense to her. "Maybe these."

There were dates and what looked like locations in the file names. She clicked one that looked like it might be the entry gate. Video of the little guard shack and the big entry gate started playing. There was a time and date stamp.

Nothing happened. Just the gate and shack for a long stretch of time. J'Leah fast-forwarded. Eventually there was a brief span when the gate opened and closed several times and cars exited.

I looked at the time stamp. "End of the day. They're going home."

"Is that interesting?"

"No." I stretched. "Wait, unless we can find Carlos. What kind of cars do you think the DeLuna brothers would drive?"

"I don't know. These are mostly sedans. Minivans. It looks like some of the employees probably have kids."

"Anything in there look distinctive?"

"You're guessing."

I was, but we looked back through the cars going out the gate. None of them got our attention. J'Leah advanced the frame slowly over the next several hours. A few vehicles went in, and a few came out, and it got dark.

I was getting bored again, and then I pointed. "Stop. Back up to the last one."

She did.

I leaned in. "What is that? And what's that emblem on the front that looks like a fishhook?"

It was a sporty car. Not overly flashy or obvious, but different enough to stand out. Like the owner of a successful company might drive to try to impress clients.

J'Leah zoomed in and the image sharpened. Royal blue, long front end that dipped steeply to a scooped grill. Sporty but with the look of some luxury.

She centered the image on the front of the car. "That's not a fish-hook. It's a trident."

"Trident?"

"Maserati." She advanced the frame and zoomed in again. "That's a Ghibli."

"Giblet?"

"Ghibli. It's the model."

"How do you know that?"

"I know a lot of things."

"You do, but cars? A Ghibli?"

"It's a desert wind."

I looked at her.

"Blows across the Libyan desert. The Mediterranean. That area."

I took out my phone.

J'Leah smiled and pointed to the Faraday cage.

I sighed and put the phone back in my pocket.

"You can check later if you don't believe me."

"I believe you. I'm just wondering how you can know so much."

She looked at me as if she was deciding something. "I've been there. In that desert. The Ghibli wind blows sand everywhere. Into your ears and mouth. And other orifices, if you let it. Sand gets between your teeth and pops when you try to chew."

"Doesn't sound like much fun."

"Nothing much I was doing when I was in that desert was fun. That left time to look up things. Like the Ghibli. Which leads to—"

"The car. I get it." And I was impressed again. I focused on the image on the screen. "Think we can find out if it's Carlos inside?"

"You're fishing."

"I am."

But she was already moving the video time index back. The car reversed as if it were backing through the gate. The car was kind of cool. It looked kind of fast. It was a Maserati. I said, "You think it'll do one eighty-five?"

She paused. Then said, "Why does that matter?"

"It's because—I…" I sighed, very deeply. "Never mind."

She froze the image and zoomed. "There's the driver."

We both looked, and we both knew. It was Carlos.

J'Leah zoomed in more until the image became pixelated and blurry. But it still looked like Carlos. She re-sharpened the image. "Is that useful?"

"Probably not. Just snooping."

I didn't want to admit it. I hadn't expected to find his car. But now that I had, the seed of an idea in my head was growing fast. There were no plates on the front of the car. I tried to sound casual. "Can we get a look at the back of the Ghibli?"

J'Leah already knew we could. She was moving the time index around. "You mean like to get a look at the plates?"

"Hmm. Now that you mention it."

"Uh-huh."

She already knew what I was going to do. Follow that Ghibli.

14

I STEPPED OUT OF THE FARADAY CAGE and turned my phone on. It lit up with missed texts. I read through them and got the gist.

Cali and Marzi had made a curry of sweet potato and tofu. Cali sent pictures. Marzi wanted me to be there. I supposed that Cali did too. There was still time.

Brick was looking for Quando and wanted Elizabeth Winstrop's number. I started with him. Easy. I sent Elizabeth's number. Maybe he'd get another slice of pie.

My fingers hovered over the phone while I considered Marzi and Cali. On my way? Save some for me? A smiley face and an ETA?

I couldn't do it. I sent a frowny face and *Working late* to both of them.

Why did I do that? Why couldn't I just join them and be happy? What was wrong with the human race that we so consistently failed to choose the thing that would make us happy and instead opted for the thing that would make us a little crazy?

My thinking was a little soft, but my brain was trying to tease a pattern out of recent events. The lines went something like this: Elizabeth Winstrop spends twenty years convincing herself that she's happy her lousy daughter ran away and she doesn't have to deal with her. Then she's reunited with her daughter and realizes family and pie are the best things in the world. Easy. Happy. That's great. What took her so long?

Then the guy in the Chevelle. Probably tooling around the house when Brick and I went past. Maybe out doing some yard work. Or watching a little TV. Maybe having a snack or a cup of coffee after work. Some salted peanuts on the porch, whatever he did to unwind after work. Or he's camped out waiting, lying in ambush. Then we drive by and the guy is so keyed up he comes out to run us off the road. To keep his daughter safe. Right when school is letting out and the buses are coming through. And Brick is reaching beneath the seat for his weapon.

I mean, the guy's got a point. But there's got to be a better way, right? Why give in to crazy? Put a sign out front that says *Drive like your grandma is crossing the street*, or *Smile, you're on camera*. Or put in a speed bump.

The thinking extended to Cali. OK, Cali was a mystery. She didn't want me to even think about another woman after her mother died, and now she's unhappy that I'm not trying to move Marzi in tonight and maybe start right away working on getting her a little brother? How hard was it to just enjoy the moments that were unfolding?

Then that line of thinking honed right in on me. I should be heading home to dinner, but I wasn't. I was letting the crazy get me. I'd been perfectly happy to walk away from the CDE thing, then Carlos fires me and I can't get out of my head that I have to try to pin something on him, I don't even know what. I should go home and follow my bliss.

But I didn't. I drove to my office.

When I got to Yellow Springs, the little village was quiet. Streetlights dropped circles of light onto empty pavement and sidewalks.

It was the witching hour. That time in the late evening when the shops were closed and restaurants wanted to be. When the bars and eateries were pushing those last few hungry lingerers off so they could close up and go home.

I inched down Xenia Avenue looking for signs of life. A lone figure threw a long shadow that angled out from the lights in front of Tom's Market. The shadow moved to the edge of the building and disappeared.

Farther down, another silent figure stood by a sedan at the corner gas station, pumping fuel under the muted lights. The bicyclers and buskers and bench-sitters had gone home. The tourists were held at bay, waiting for daybreak when the village would reawaken. It was a part of the day here that I appreciated, except for one important inconvenience. I was hungry.

The kitchen at Peach's Grill would be closed. Miguel's Tacos would be cleaning up. The Sunrise Cafe and the Winds Cafe would be done with the dinner service. It was the witching hour, and I was witched.

The light still burned on the mast above Ye Olde Trail Tavern. I greedily eyed movement behind the window, and I wedged the truck in at the curb and hurried over.

A couple of people sat outside at the fire pit over glasses of beer. Two others sat inside at the old wooden bar. A woman worked behind the bar, restocking the coolers with bottled beer. The TV on the wall silently played a game show. My eyes shifted. The window to the kitchen still had its lights on.

I sat on a stool near the woman working. "Kitchen still open?"

She looked over at a young guy with pageboy hair and a lot of energy. He was dancing to something jangly coming from the jukebox.

I said, "To go," and the guy heard me and nodded back to the bartender.

She smiled. "If you order right now." Her hand went below the bar and came up with a menu that she placed in front of me.

I waved the menu off. "Veggie burger?"

She nodded. "What side?"

"Slaw?"

She nodded again and tapped the order into a screen. The guy who was a good dancer had heard and was already back in the kitchen hustling out the order.

The woman said, "Five minutes, maybe a few more."

I sat on the stool.

"Time for a beer if you're thirsty."

I was. It was September, and they had a Marzen. Oktoberfest beer. Better get one now or a whole calendar would go by before I had another chance. But I was ditching Cali and Marzi for a fool's errand. My brain itched with that fool's errand. I wanted to be sharp. I pointed to the TV. "How about just the remote? Can we switch to the ball game?"

No one else was watching. The two other guys at the bar were picking up to leave.

She palmed the remote. "Football?"

I shook my head. "Reds."

She flicked through the menu until the Cincinnati baseball game came up. It was the end of the season and down to the wire and the Reds were battling for a playoff spot.

I settled in for a couple of plays. Bottom of the inning at a home game. Two on, second and third. Two outs. Two-and-two count. Two-seam fastball, down and in.

Joey Votto swung and lifted the ball to shallow center. It died fast and looked like it would dink into no-man's land for a hit. The Minnesota fielder closed at full speed. He couldn't get there. He dove, eyes watching the ball as he crashed to the turf. The ball dropped into the leather and stuck. Six more inches of field and there would be joy in Mudville. But it looked like the Twins for the playoffs.

The players left the field. I dropped my head to the rows and rows of pennies embedded in epoxy that made up the top of the bar. I ran my finger along the neat lines, looking for a wheat penny.

The game came back on. No wheat penny. There never was. I waved the bartender over. "About that beer."

The place was empty. She had my order in her hand. "Food's ready."

I sighed and gave her my credit card. It was a night of missed opportunities. No playoffs, no wheat penny, no beer.

I crossed the street and went up to my office. Opened the carryout carton and pulled the top off the veggie burger. I dumped the coleslaw on top. All that was missing was a bottle of Ski. Kentucky Headhunters, eat your heart out.

I felt better when the burger was down. A little office with a window and the best view of the village is sweeter when your tummy is full.

Then I got to work on my laptop. It was a simple task, something I could have done at home. But if I was home when Cali got in, she would wonder why I hadn't gone over to Marzi's. I would wonder too. What I wanted to do could wait until morning. It could wait until never. But the itch in my frontal cortex was scratching like a loose thread.

I went to the Greene County Auditor's website. Navigated to the property search page. Entered Carlos DeLuna's name. Nothing came up.

I tried just DeLuna. Names and property addresses came up, but none with Carlos attached. There were none with Carlos as a middle name, and none with anything close to Carlos as a first name. Nothing with the initial C.

I tried the same thing with Drummond. Nothing. Judy, Carlos' wife's name. Nothing.

I went to the Montgomery County property search and started over there. I got the same result. That's when I looked up a map of Ohio counties and started working more methodically.

I moved south first. Clinton County. Warren County.

I moved up to Miami County.

From there I thought maybe Carlos was a big-city guy. It wasn't unusual for people to commute an hour from Cincinnati or Columbus. I tried Columbus. Franklin County, Madison, Delaware. I didn't find Carlos.

I was resigned to searching counties in the Cincinnati area next, but I was losing faith and already thinking of other strategies. I could search for court records, claims, rulings, deeds, property transfers, anything that might lead to an address for Carlos DeLuna if the property search didn't work.

It didn't seem likely that Carlos would not own a home somewhere in the area. Maybe he'd put it in his wife's maiden name. I could look for marriage records, but Carlos and Judy might have gotten married in Mexico, or just about anywhere else. I could be here a while.

I looked back at the map of Ohio counties and wondered if I'd missed something. I ticked them off Greene, Clark—had I looked in Clark County?

I hadn't. Turns out, Carlos was a Springfield guy. So was his brother Drummond. They both owned homes in Clark County.

I looked at the property sketch for Carlos' place, the sale date, past sales, purchase amount, and tax records. Both Carlos and Drummond were up to date on paying their property taxes. For whatever that knowledge was worth.

I looked up Carlos's house on Google street view. The grounds were kept up nice, with professional landscaping. Brick walkways and mulched trees and flowerbeds. Pots flowing over with plants lining the porch and walkways. A two-car garage with a dormer room over.

I searched up the property on Zillow. The sale price there matched what the county site said Carlos had paid.

I clicked on the photo gallery. The interior images were several years old and from a former owner, but it was real nice inside. Open floor plan downstairs, with a big kitchen and granite countertops. Shiny new appliances. High ceilings with elongated skylights. Oriole windows on the front wall.

Not things I'd look for in a house, but that wasn't important. I just wanted to know that I had him.

I swiveled in my chair and looked out my office window. The village below had gotten even quieter. The lights were out at the tavern. The stoplight at the corner changed to green, and a single set of headlights moved south on Xenia Avenue below me.

I tried not to feel melancholy. I hardly ever did. Or I hardly ever did before I lost my wife. Something like that brings on melancholy, and worse. But this feeling wasn't about my lost wife. It was about the here and now. Tonight. And I'd brought it on myself. Finding Carlos was satisfying, but was I happier than if I'd spent the evening with Marzi and Cali?

15

I WAS TERRIBLE AT STAKEOUTS. Sitting still for me is about as exciting as standing in front of the bakery window watching the bread rise. I get bored, and I get hungry. And I like coffee. I'd heard stories of guys taking a plastic bottle and such on stakeouts so they could sit for a long time without leaving the mark. I wasn't one of those guys.

Like I said, I'm not good at stakeouts.

It might have been some motivation if I had a good reason to follow Carlos. But it felt mostly like spite. I didn't let that stop me.

After Cali was off to school, I texted J'Leah.

Her reply came a few minutes later. *Early.*

Sun's been up for an hour.

Good news waits until noon.

Not today. I need a GPS tracker.

Lots of them on Amazon.

Hoping to have one in hand today.

Used to be this store called Radio Shack. Maybe there's one still open you can find.

I opened a browser on my phone.

It was as if J'Leah knew what I was doing. *You're not really looking for a Radio Shack?*

Well I'm not now.

Walmart. Best Buy. I'm looking these up on my phone right now. You can do the same thing.

You're kidding? Walmart?

I'll send you a link.

I was kind of hoping someone would show me how to use it too.

Folks at Walmart could do that.

Folks at Walmart aren't as smart as you.

If a text could convey a sigh, J'Leah's next one did. *You want me to help you?*

Yes, please. When I didn't get a reply right away, I added, *Do I need to stop somewhere and buy one?*

No. Don't get that junk off the shelf. I have something better.

Now we're talking. *Meet for coffee?*

At least.

We agreed on the Sunrise Cafe. I went to get us a table.

When J'Leah arrived, she picked up a menu and perused. A moment later the waitress came over and asked if we knew what we wanted.

I did. "Jackson Flint breakfast special."

J'Leah laughed. "No one knows what that means."

"Of course they don't. Just bring me the breakfast sampler. No meat."

"How would you like your eggs?"

"Surprise me."

"Toast, biscuit, or English muffin?"

"Whatever is your favorite."

She nodded but didn't tell me what her favorite was. Perfect. It wouldn't spoil the surprise.

I added, "And a coffee."

"Cream?"

I grinned.

She said, "I'll surprise you."

J'Leah was still touring the menu. "This is on you?"

"And my expense account."

"I can't decide between the veggie scramble and the huevos rancheros."

"Then don't."

She looked up. "What?"

"Don't decide. Get both."

"I can't eat all that."

"You can get a box."

"Why would I do that?" J'Leah looked to the waitress.

The waitress said, "Or I can surprise you."

J'Leah sighed, nodded, and closed her menu.

Then we chatted over coffee until breakfast arrived. Surprise. The waitress brought both the veggie scramble and the huevos rancheros for J'Leah.

I got an egg sunny side up with onions and peppers on top, and an English muffin. Score.

J'Leah gave an exasperated look at the two plates in front of her.

I said, "I understand you young people don't like to cook so much."

She speared a broccoli floret and some egg. "I'll have you know that I'm a terrific cook. It's your generation that learned to eat out of microwaves."

True enough. We ate, J'Leah moving between the two plates. When she slowed down, the waitress came back and said, "Anything else?"

I winked. "Pumpkin pancake."

J'Leah groaned. "How do you not weigh three hundred pounds?"

"Nobody knows."

The pancake came a few minutes later and I cut it in half.

J'Leah gave me the stink eye. "No way."

I pushed half the flapjack onto one of her plates. "You won't regret it."

She ate the pancake. Or tried to. I don't know if she regretted it.

I paid the tab, and J'Leah toted her takeout box. Her little Bolt was parked at the street. She opened the hatch and dug into one of a series of black zippered bags stored there. She extracted what she wanted, tucked that into her backpack, and we went up to my office.

She was sitting behind my desk before I had my key out of the door. I yielded and opened one of the small folding chairs that leaned against the wall. "Are you comfortable there?"

"Peachy." She had a small device on the desk. "You know how this works?"

"GPS tracker. Gets signals from three different satellites and triangulates location."

"Right. I mean in user terms. Have you ever used one?"

"Oh. No."

She frowned. "In your line of work?"

"I've never been good at stakeouts."

"With this it's not a stakeout. It does most of the work for you."

"I guess I never thought of it that way."

She frowned again. "People use these for everything. Luggage, dogs, their kids. Bicycles."

"Yeah."

"It seems like something you would have found a use for."

I thought about it. There was no way I was going to sneak one into Cali's pack or ask her to carry one. Bicycles disappeared in town fairly often, so that might be useful. Sometimes I wondered where Mrs. Jenkins wandered off to in the night. I refocused. When would it have been useful for work? "Can it track a sandwich?"

"A sandwich?"

"When I was a county deputy, someone would steal my lunch from the fridge. Once or twice a month it would disappear. I'd liked to have caught the person who was taking my sandwiches."

"Sure, Jackson, it could track a sandwich. If you had some way to keep the tag with the sandwich."

I thought about it. I could do that.

J'Leah stared. "Focus. Give me your phone."

I did.

She turned the tracker on and tapped my phone.

I reached over. "You have to swipe like this to get in." I made a motion with my finger.

"I know how to get into your phone."

"How do you—"

She rolled her eyes and unlocked my phone. "I'm installing an app for the tracker."

"I could probably figure out how to do that."

"Anybody could. Just watch the Amazon video." She finished the install, turned the phone around, and ran through the functions. It didn't take long.

I picked up the tracker. There wasn't much to it. "How long will the battery last?"

"About two weeks. Longer than you should be fooling around with this, which is not at all."

She was right. I hefted the thing in a palm. "It's magnetic?"

She showed me by sticking it to the metal filing cabinet. "So you're going to put it on the Ghibli?"

"I'm not going to break into the CDE compound again. That would be B&E now that the contract is terminated. In Ohio, tracking someone isn't currently illegal. I'll try for the Ghibli."

She frowned. "This would be simpler if you just tracked his phone. And he'd probably have that with him all the time."

"You mean spyware?"

"Easy. You just drive behind him. When he turns his Wi-Fi or Bluetooth on, which he will, I can hack his signal."

"Now that would be illegal."

She pushed up from my chair. "It would. I can't believe you even have me thinking like this." She waved a hand. "Take that thing and go."

"But it's my office."

She grabbed her backpack. "Then I'll go."

I tucked the tracker into my pocket. Now if I could just get the thing onto the Ghibli.

The itch in my head called. One scratch at a time, Jackson.

16

STAKING OUT CARLOS was worse than I thought. Even getting the tracker on his car was painful.

I waited outside the CDE compound. It was a warm autumn day, and that meant bugs. Mosquitoes and wasps and bees and stink bugs and pollinators and flying crawling and stinging things of all sorts were in full bore searching for winter digs. Every crack, crevice, and hollow where they could crawl or fly in and wait out the freeze was a target.

I don't mind bugs generally, and I go out of my way to let the pollinators and native critters be the part of nature they are designed for. But with the truck windows down, mosquitoes were buzzing in. An industrious wasp nosed in. I rolled the windows up, and I created climate change right there in the cab of my truck. Too hot.

I gave up and left the windows down, slapping occasionally.

It was interesting that I found myself in a cemetery again, and it wasn't the place I'd parked the night I broke into the CDE compound. But it was close enough that I could make out the shape of the CDE buildings across the soy fields.

With the binoculars I could pick out the lot of cars inside the compound gate, and away from them up beside the farmhouse, the Ghibli. If the terrain had been flatter and I had a better pair of binoculars, I might have been able to see a third cemetery down the road. The three were like GPS satellites, triangulating around the CDE compound to gain a fix on it.

Do you know how many cemeteries there are in Clark and Greene Counties in Ohio? Neither did I, and apparently maybe nobody did. To pass the time, between slapping at mosquitoes, I had looked them up. Some websites listed a couple of dozen cemeteries per county. Other sites listed more, both still operating or no longer used. Google maps showed cemeteries not listed anywhere else I could find. How does a cemetery get on Google maps but not on a county website?

I found pictures and descriptions of most of the smaller graveyards. I looked at them on Google street view. Some you wouldn't know if you drove right past them. Several looked like they were on old family farms or plots of land. A few were named the same as the road they were on, which probably meant both the road and the cemetery were named for a family who lived there back in the day when the settlers were still pushing into lands where the natives had lived.

Some of the cemeteries had roads or entries that looked passable if not well kept. Others were buried deep in farm fields and away from access or curious eyes. A fair number had no roads or walkways. They were simply a collection of graves either off the road or next to an old house or withered chapel that looked out of use.

That's where I was, off road in the grass at the edge of the tombstones and beneath a line of trees that had once been a stately overture to the solemn grounds beyond. There was no road or trace of old road. Maybe there never had been. I had simply slowed the truck and driven off the blacktop and onto the grass. From there I circled behind the remains of an old brick chapel and parked along the tombstones, angled out toward the fields beyond.

The cemeteries were more interesting than the stakeout, and I almost missed the Ghibli when it appeared on the road.

Now I needed some luck. I followed. Carlos drove too slowly for a car as sporty as the Ghibli. Hey, it's a Maserati. I don't think I could have kept my foot out of the pedal. But Carlos puttered like he wasn't sure where he was going. Maybe he wasn't sure. When he stopped for gas, I got my luck.

Carlos filled the tank. Then he went into the station store, I went to the Ghibli, and the tracker went underneath. I got back in the truck and pulled away onto a residential street and watched the dot on my phone.

A few minutes later, the dot moved. So did I. I followed that dot all the way to Carlos' house, where the garage door opened, the Ghibli pulled in, and the garage door closed. That was it.

Now what?

I had no idea, so I waited. Nothing happened except I got bored and hungry. So I went home. That's what the tracker was for, right?

But the itch had a firm grip on me. I'd already wasted most of a day sitting in a cemetery slapping at bugs. Then I wasted most of a night checking my phone and staring at the little dot that never moved from Carlos' garage.

In the morning it started all over again. Every time the Ghibli moved, I jumped in the truck and headed to intercept it. I spent a lot of time driving to and from the CDE compound and a couple of trips to Carlos' office near the Air Force base.

The whole time I kept telling myself Jackson, just eat some pie. Relax. Go home. Stop this.

I was tired of it on the first day. I was ready to quit on the second. I did on the third.

It was Friday. I'd followed Carlos to his home to pick up his wife, then into Dayton where he'd gone to one of my favorite places: the Wheat Penny restaurant.

It was a sign. The wheat penny. I didn't ignore the message. Quando had thrown his wheat penny away into the woods. I wasn't going to throw mine away. I walked across the parking lot to the Ghibli and in one quick motion bent and retrieved the tracker.

I'd tossed the itch away. Now if I could get my bliss back.

I texted Marzi. *Dinner tonight?*

It took her a few minutes to answer. *Still at work. Kind of late notice.*

I'm in Dayton. You could meet me.

Where are you?

I sent emojis of a shaft of wheat and a coin.

??

I sent an emoji of bread.

???

I gave up and texted *Wheat Penny.*

That did it. I got *Oooooh. 20 minutes.*

Welcome back, bliss.

I didn't even care if Carlos saw me. A good P.I. didn't like coincidences. But tonight I just wanted to be Jackson. I wanted my wheat penny. I went in and got a seat at the bar.

That put my back to the interior. I caught a glimpse on my way in of Carlos sitting at a table with his back to me. A woman sat with him. They were dressed up like they were having a night out. Good for them.

I let it go and turned to the drink menu. A young guy dressed in black and with a sharp haircut and clean shave appeared. "Something to your liking?"

"All of it."

"We get that a lot. Think you can narrow it down some?"

"Anything from the Yellow Springs Brewery."

He reached to a cooler beneath the bar top and placed a tall clean glass and a can of beer in front of me. "Anything else look good?"

I poured the beer into the glass. "I'll start with this. I'm waiting on a lady."

He winked. "We get that a lot here too."

I sipped. The beer was crisp. A citrus IPA. Not too hoppy. Excellent. I lifted the glass again, and the brew washed away the Ghibli. Washed away the CDE compound, Carlos DeLuna, the shenanigans. Another sip washed away any lingering thoughts of the scabs that had nearly healed on my back and legs. All gone.

And just like that, so was the beer.

I raised an arm to the bartender and asked for another. Then I remembered the Lawrence Block paperback I still had in my jacket pocket, and I wondered if it would look cool to read a book while I sat at the bar and waited for a lady. I decided it would, but I didn't want to make all the other guys there without books look less cool, so I kept mine in my pocket.

I looked through the menu, thought about Marzi, and thought about Cali. Then I gave in and took the book out and started reading. I figured the others could take it.

I was almost through the denouement when I felt a whisper at my elbow and Marzi at the stool beside me.

I stuffed the book back in my jacket and stood to pull out Marzi's stool. "Waiting on a table."

She hung her jacket on the back of the stool. "Good book?"

"It is."

"Looked like you were just about done."

"Just a few more pages."

"You want to finish?"

I shook my head. "No. I've been waiting for you."

It must have been a good answer. Marzi smiled. Silver earrings with tiny mermaids danced from her ears. Her work clothes still looked fresh and she smelled good. How did women do that?

The bartender came back and gave his full attention to Marzi. "Ah, the lady has arrived." He smiled big, palms flat on the bar and his gaze on Marzi. "Is there something I can get for you?"

Marzi winked at me. "I like him."

The guy didn't blush, blink, or bat at eye. He knew what he was doing. He kept his attention on Marzi.

Marzi looked at my empty glass. "Looks like you were having beer."

Beers. I didn't correct her. Instead I waved off the cocktail menu. "If I might make a recommendation?"

She was agreeable.

"Kate's whiskey sour."

Marzi tipped her head.

"Best you'll ever get." It felt flirty, and the look on Marzi's face said she must have thought so too.

She nodded to the bartender.

He was already reaching for the cocktail shaker. "Excellent choice." He mixed, and his eyes went to my empty glass.

I tapped a finger on the bar. "Same, unless you can mix a foxpossum."

He looked confused.

Marzi didn't. She patted my hand. "Nobody knows what that is. You made that drink up."

The sharp-dressed bartender shook and strained Marzi's drink, tipped the last of the foamy egg white on top, then speared a Luxardo cherry with a fancy toothpick and laid that across the rim of the glass.

He pushed the glass to Marzi and watched her while she sipped.

Marzi took a dainty taste. "Very nice."

The guy set another beer in front of me. "Just for my edification, what's a foxpossum?"

I lifted an eyebrow.

"Yeah, I've been to college and learned some fancy words." He wiped the bar with a towel. "This pays better."

I sipped the new beer. "Cheers to that. A foxpossum is an elusive cocktail that has a slippery recipe usually consisting of homemade gin, homemade sour cherry liqueur, lime, sometimes bergamot, and lots of ice."

He thought about it. "We could get about as far as the ice and lime. After that, I think you'd be on your own." Then he moved away down the bar.

Marzi straightened on her stool. "I was a bit surprised to hear from you tonight."

I shrugged. It didn't seem to impress her. I tried something else. "Sorry. I've been distracted."

"You have."

It was kind of her. I'd been absent. I tried to catch her eye. "I think I'm back now."

"Oh?" She watched me lift my beer again. "And what have you been distracted by?"

"Some wrinkles with my work."

Her look told me that was a woefully insufficient answer.

"I'll tell you," I said. "But first I want to tell you a story."

A twinkle came into her eye. "I like stories."

"This one is about a wheat penny."

The twinkle brightened. Marzi turned on her barstool so she was facing me and her legs bumped against mine. "Go on."

Just then the bartender came and said, "Table's ready." He pointed to the hostess station where a woman stood holding menus. "She'll take you. I can send your drinks over."

Marzi tilted her head and looked at the guy. A silver earring dangled from behind her amber brown hair. "It's so cozy here. Might we stay at the bar to eat?"

She didn't have to convince him. The bartender waved the hostess off and dropped menus on the bar in front of us. "I'd be delighted."

Marzi tilted back to me. "Did I say I like him?"

The guy didn't even try to pretend he hadn't heard.

Marzi let her menu sit on the bar. "Tell me about the wheat penny."

I took a breath. "I'll give you the short version." And I told her about Quando finding a wheat penny. How the job with Carlos DeLuna had gone sideways. We were fired. It bothered me, but I thought about the wheat penny and realized I just wanted to try to be happy. It was a metaphor. I invited her to dinner. That made me happy. End of short version of the story.

Marzi took a careful sip from her whiskey sour and returned her glass to the cocktail napkin. "Now I think you should tell me the longer version."

The beer kept me talking. I gave her the whole thing. Musing about why people seem to want to make themselves unhappy. My itch to find something on Carlos DeLuna. I threw in a bit about the guy in the Chevelle. Why was it so hard to find a little thing that could make you happy enough? Just the wheat penny, that's all I needed. The wheat penny that Quando threw away into the woods, and this one here, the Wheat Penny restaurant. And her, Marzi. Then I could be happy.

It sounded a little sloppy at the end. My beer was almost gone. Had I drunk two before Marzi got here or three?

Like the good counselor that she was, Marzi listened without comment. Then she picked up her menu. "I'd like to hear more, especially about that last part. But first let's get some food in front of us."

Good idea.

The bartender in black saw us look at the menus and sensed it was time to come back.

Marzi laid her menu down. "The mussels look good."

The guy looked at me and grinned.

Then I got it. I grinned back.

Marzi's eyes said she didn't understand.

I raised an arm and flexed a bicep. "Muscles, coming right up."

She rolled her eyes. Boys.

The bartender went with it. He pointed to me. "Double order of mussels for you?"

I waved him off. "Portobello sandwich."

He looked a little disappointed that the joke was over. "Greens or jojos?"

"Jojos. I'll be good tomorrow."

He tapped the order into a screen.

I added, "Caesar salad and the squash and shitakes to share."

"Anchovies on the salad?"

I looked to Marzi.

She waved a hand yes.

"Let 'em swim."

The guy smiled. "Refills?"

I wanted to say yes. Instead I said, "Long drive home."

Marzi held her hand over her glass. "I'll just have the one." She looked at me for a second. "I can drive you home. Have another beer."

"But my truck is here."

"We'll come back for it."

"Kind of a long drive."

She leaned in. "Jackson, have another beer. Trust me, I'll make it worth your while."

I pointed to my glass, but the bartender was already reaching for a new one.

I started in on another beer. How many was that?

Thankfully, the salad came early. Marzi and I squared off with the plate between us. I raised my fork. "Thanks for going with the anchovies. Cali worries that I make weird foods when you come over."

"You do."

"I do?"

"That's part of your charm."

I liked the sound of that, and I didn't ask what part of me that made up.

We dug into the salad and swimmers, and Marzi said, "So he's here now?"

"Huh?"

"Carlos. You said you followed him. That's why you were here."

I'd forgotten. Which was the point. I pulled my eyes to my right. Carlos was still there. "Three tables over. Back is to us. He's wearing a jacket."

Marzi was very discreet. She pushed some hair behind one ear and in that motion stole a look. "Wife has the nice jewelry?"

"That's him."

"And he hasn't seen you?"

"Much as I can tell."

She chewed some greenery. "You don't look worried that he might see you."

"Like I said, I've moved on."

She almost looked convinced. Then our dinners arrived to distract us from further discussion of the question.

A few minutes into my portobello sandwich, my phone buzzed. I read a text, tapped a reply, and pushed the phone back into my pocket.

Marzi watched me over her mussels. "Cali?"

"Yeah. She's with friends. I told her I was out with you." I lifted my beer, set it back down again. "She said I didn't have a curfew."

Marzi knew it was a joke, but the counselor in her was alert. She placed her fork along the edge of her plate. "This is going to be complicated for Cali for a while. She's still adjusting to the loss of her mother. She's deep into adolescence. Her friends are older and they're already planning to leave her for college. She wants stability, and you and I can't promise exactly what's to come. In many ways."

Spoken like a true counselor.

She put a hand on my knee. "That doesn't mean we can't take our time to figure things out. And we can enjoy ourselves tonight while we do that."

Uh, waiter? Check, please. I wasn't going to throw this wheat penny away.

And just when things were really sailing nicely, right then two men caught my eye at the door. They wore black suits and stood talking intensely with the hostess. One of the men looked about the restaurant and touched the elbow of the other. Then they turned and walked straight to Carlos DeLuna's table.

I tried very hard not to care.

The men reached Carlos and he greeted them as if he had expected their arrival. Coffee and a dessert sat on the table between Carlos and his wife.

Carlos rose. One of the men took the seat Carlos had been in and engaged in conversation with Carlos' wife. Carlos and the other man walked out of the restaurant.

Well, damn. I tried really hard not to be interested. But the beer was still talking, and my brain wasn't entirely listening to reason.

I set my napkin on the bar. "Be right back."

Marzi looked up.

I pointed to my empty beer glass.

She understood.

I started for the restrooms, checked that Marzi wasn't looking, and veered for the door.

I didn't think about it. There wasn't time.

I stepped outside. Across the parking lot, Carlos and the man in the black suit got into the Ghibli. I hurried around the perimeter of the lot to the truck, reached in, and found the tracker.

A handful of seconds later, I had come around the perimeter again and dropped behind a hedge at the street. I was exposed to traffic but shielded from the Ghibli, and from there I crouched low and punched a hand through the greenery, felt the car, and stuck the tracker on.

I was back inside and in the restroom and back to the bar with Marzi a minute later. If she thought I'd been gone too long, she didn't let on.

The bartender came over and smiled at us. "Room for dessert?"

I deferred to Marzi.

She shook her head. "We shouldn't."

"Right."

"But if you say so, the croustade would be nice."

"Croustade?"

"If you say so." She winked at the bartender. "Pear croustade."

He swished away.

"You ordered two of them?"

Marzi turned the dessert menu placard toward me. "Pear."

"Oh. Now if I only knew what a croustade was."

It didn't take long to find out. The croustade arrived. It was a fancy pie kind of thing. Which was perfect. Jackson, just relax and eat some pie. That's what I'd been telling myself. And now here it was right in front of me. I ate.

And I picked up the check. Carlos' table was empty when we left. Sobriety was settling in, and I regretted having paid attention to Carlos and the men dressed in black at all. I didn't want to know who they were or why they'd come to talk to Carlos. I wanted to eat pie and hang with Marzi and Cali and follow my bliss.

We stopped at the door. I pointed to a photo on the shelf at the entry. "That's the chef."

Marzi squinted at the old black-and-white picture. "How do you know that?"

"It's from a long time ago. She told me once that it reminded her of a simpler time, when happiness was easier to find but harder to recognize."

Marzi was silent for a moment. "Like Quando's penny."

"Like Quando's penny. Which he threw away."

"But the penny wasn't happiness for him. It was for you."

I let out a breath. "If things were only that simple."

Marzi took my hand. "Tonight, for a little while, maybe they can be."

17

MARZI WANTED A WALK, so we left the Wheat Penny and strolled downtown Dayton. Wandered Wayne Avenue past the Dublin Pub and the Troll Pub. Went under the railroad tracks and passed a block away from Warped Wing Brewery. Turned at the Barrel House and walked in front of the Dayton Beer Company. Made a right at the baseball stadium and passed the Moeller Brew Barn, Brixx Ice Company, and the Local Cantina. Turned at Webster Street and flanked the Little Fish Brewing Company.

I noticed a pattern. Beer trail. I was sobering up, so I didn't point that out.

We meandered the length of the 2nd Street Market. It called to my mind the case from the past summer that had brought me to Elizabeth Winstrop, and that made me think of searching for Elizabeth's daughter and finding she had a granddaughter. And now that granddaughter was living in Yellow Springs and going to the same school as my own daughter.

And now Quando was in the mix. And Angelita Rojas Flores, from another case last summer, had something going with Brick. Put that together with Cali moving in the same circles as Willow Winstrop and Quando, and that Elizabeth had referred Carlos DeLuna to me, and it looked like my work was sending out ripples that were intersecting the ripples of my personal life. Some strange kind of convergence.

I nudged Marzi down the Ford Street alley. We emerged at the shiny new library. Willow and Henna Winstrop had followed these routes. I had followed them on these streets, and that had brought them together back in our little village. I felt some satisfaction thinking I'd done some good.

By the time we got back to the Wheat Penny and our vehicles, my head had cleared and we decided we'd both drive back to Yellow Springs. I followed Marzi to her place. We went inside to share some quality time.

Then I'd gone home to my own bed and fallen asleep. I woke later when Cali came home. It was a reasonable hour. I heard her bump around, water running in the bathroom, then her bedroom door creak.

Mrs. Jenkins was curled beside me and raised her head to listen. Then she stretched and plopped off the bed and padded out my door. A moment later I heard the soft meow of the cat offering her head for Cali to rub.

I fell back asleep and dreamed I was in a small boat on a large calm pond. Gentle ripples moved me slowly about on the surface of the water. Other boats came into view, then neared, but in circuitous, indirect pathways. Sometimes another boat would drift close and follow the same path as mine for a little while. Always there was someone I knew in the other boats, but it was a dream and the images weren't clear and I could never tell exactly who I was travelling with. It wasn't the worst dream ever.

Cali was asleep when I woke in the morning. I put on my shoes and went for a run through the village. My legs were loose and carried me quickly. I ran and watched my little burg wake up on a sleepy Saturday morning.

I cruised past the farmer's market. It was sprinkled with late-season sellers and shoppers. I ran on. The coffee shops were filled with people who had time to linger on a weekend morning, and a busker with a rhythm guitar warmed up in the chill air in front of Asanda Imports.

I stopped at the Emporium and went in for coffee, a breakfast burrito, and a rosemary salt biscuit. Then I added a ginger muffin and a Chelsea roll. Why not? My bank account was flush.

I walked home. On the way, I drank the coffee and started on the ginger muffin. Cali was up when I got back, and we had breakfast together at the little table in the kitchen with what was left of the bounty from the Emporium.

Now I was back in my office above the village, finishing a few tasks I wanted to put behind me. Itemizing some expense account items and making a few notes about the DeLuna case that I planned to file away forever.

I never once checked the GPS tracker from my phone, and I didn't plan to.

I finished the tasks and rocked back in my chair to look out my window. The sun was canting in on the village from the sharp, low angle that happens only in the autumn, making the street below appear as if it were lit from below rather than above. Everything glowed. It was a very good morning.

Then the guys in black suits arrived.

There were footsteps outside the door, then a shiny pair of black shoes appeared as someone figured out to step past the door that was hung backward, open it, then step back through. Another pair of shiny black shoes as the second guy figured it out.

Then the shoes were connected to pressed black pants, charcoal gray shirts, and black jackets. No ties.

Both of the men wore short, crisp haircuts and had wide shoulders. One looked older at late thirties or early forties. The other looked like he was just out of the academy and still paying for his first suit. It didn't take me long to figure maybe it was the guys who'd met Carlos DeLuna at the Wheat Penny the night before.

The men jockeyed for space in my little office. I watched them and said, "There's more room with the door open."

They figured that out. The younger of the two backed into the doorway and stood against the frame.

I asked if they'd like to sit.

They would.

I pointed to the folding chairs. The man inside took one, unfolded it, and sat. That took up most of the space across from my desk.

The younger man tried to reach around for the other chair, gave up, and went back to standing in the door frame. His partner didn't seem bothered by the other guy being left out there.

The guy in the chair spoke first. "Mister Flint?"

"Present."

"Jackson Flint?"

"Guilty."

Now the guy in the door got in on it. "Jackson W. Flint?"

I sighed. "Only to my mother."

He was looking at something printed on a half-sheet of paper. "Whetstone? Says here your middle name is Whetstone."

"From my mother's family." I leaned toward them over my desk, spread my arms out, and touched the ends of my fingers together. Trying to be as large as possible and take up as much oxygen and space in the room as I could. "We've established who I am. Jackson Whetstone Flint. The question now is who the two of you are, and why you are in my office."

The guy in the door said, "We're representatives of the federal—"

The other raised a hand to stop him. "FBI. You've probably guessed that by now. You may have seen me and another of my associates at a location in Dayton, Ohio last night."

"At a location…?"

He nodded, sort of. His chin dipped, or his eyes blinked, or something to show that he was alive and listening. "In Dayton."

"You mean the Wheat Penny."

"The location has not been disclosed."

But we both knew where he meant. Interesting, the feds. I said, "You were the one who kept company with DeLuna's wife while the other guy in a suit went out and had a talk with him."

"Correct. I'm agent Kaufman." He jerked a thumb over his shoulder without turning to look. "And this is my associate, Mister Anderson."

I tried to stop the grin from coming, but this was too good. I laced my fingers together and turned them around and cracked my knuckles. "Mister Anderson." I drew the syllables out long.

They didn't get it. I wondered if they'd laugh if I asked if they were going to flashy-thingy me. I didn't do it. If the feds don't think you're funny, it's probably a losing game to keep trying to make the point.

Kaufman said, "Mister Flint, if you will—"

"IDs." I tapped a finger on my desk. Neither of them had offered to shake. That was just rude. Now I was going to make them work for it.

Kaufman said, "I don't believe—"

"IDs." I tapped again.

Kaufman reached to the breast pocket of his suit and pulled a wallet out. "I assure you that we are with the Federal Bureau of Investigations."

"Oh, I believe you."

Anderson had moved from his slouch against the doorframe. He gave me the stink-eye. I gave it back, wondering if we were going to do the Bogart dance. He didn't need to show me no stinking badge.

I didn't like it. They could connect me to Carlos DeLuna, but they could be civil about it.

Anderson crossed his arms. "If you believe us, why ask for identification?"

"Because I can."

Kaufman gave Anderson a look, and Anderson extracted a wallet similar to Kaufman's from a recess in his suit jacket. Each man's wallet held a badge and a printed identification card. They flipped their wallets open for a few seconds, then closed them again.

It didn't matter. It was a game. IDs were easy enough to forge. I had no reason to believe these were fake, and even with a close look I wouldn't be able to tell if they'd been forged. What would tell me if these guys were really with the feds was how they reacted.

"Now then," Kaufman said.

I held up a hand. With the other hand I tapped a finger on the desk again. "Let's have a closer look."

Kaufman looked surprised. He did not open his wallet again. "If you'd rather, we can do this at the regional office. I'm sure the local authorities would be quick to assist here if need be." He nodded to Anderson, who held a finger out over his phone.

There's nothing like getting into the local small-town newspaper police report for having FBI agents at your office. I planned not to. I rose and extended a hand to Kaufman. "Jackson Flint. Now that's cleared up, we can be nice."

Kaufman shook once, firmly. Now we were getting somewhere.

I extended the hand farther for Anderson. He shifted awkwardly around Kaufman to reach me. We shook once, harder than necessary, then Anderson retreated to the doorway again and looked at me like I was a jackass. Maybe I was.

I straightened my back. "And how may I assist the Federal Bureau of Investigations?"

Anderson gave a look with his eyes that said *jeez*. But Kaufman was all business. "You were hired by CDE Enterprises to do a security check of the premises in Clark County, Ohio."

I sat.

Kaufman looked at me. "Can you confirm that?"

"Look, maybe you'd better tell me what's going on. I can make some calls, maybe ascertain what extent of client privacy is due here. It would be easier if I knew what this is about."

Kaufman's face stayed perfectly composed. "This is a classified matter."

I exhaled. "My business cards indicate that I'm discreet."

Anderson snickered. Kaufman did not. He said, "This is an interview. It is not obligatory on your part. But be aware that we are pursuing a warrant for your home and personal items, including any and all electronic devices owned or used by you, your associates, or your family."

That was some serious lawyer talk. I didn't like the sound of it. And I knew Cali wouldn't like the sound of her phone and laptop being taken away. At all.

Kaufman pressed the issue. "We can be coy, Mister Flint, or we can be frank and help each other out. I think you'll find it's in your interests to do the latter. Once a warrant is secured, you'll no longer have a choice in the matter."

More with the lawyer talk. "On what grounds might a warrant be issued?"

Kaufman blinked once, then proceeded as if that had cleared some circuitry for him. "CDE is under contract with the federal government for work on certain projects. The work on those projects has disappeared. Your government would like to locate those assets and re-secure them."

We'd gone from not naming the restaurant we both knew to alluding to secret government contracts. That was a long haul. "I'm listening."

"There is a verified report of a breach and break-in at the CDE Clark County premises." Kaufman lifted a phone in his hand and swiped, looked at the screen. "That event took place six days ago. You were the person who breached the grounds."

He looked at me, waiting for a reply. I debated. Of course they might know I'd been on the grounds. Carlos could have told them that. But the FBI should also be aware that the Jackson Flint Detective Agency had a signed contract and legal grounds for the breach. And there was client privacy. But these were the feds. Some lines could get blurred.

What I decided was to give Kaufman a nod.

That was enough. He went on. "You were also contracted as part of that arrangement to complete a cyber security detail check of the CDE systems."

I nodded again. I didn't like where this was headed, but they already knew.

"Drummond DeLuna now claims that the missing materials disappeared the night of the breach, at the time when you were inside the CDE boundary and on the premises."

Wait. The night I went into the compound? J'Leah hadn't done anything by then.

"DeLuna further claims that—"

"Wait. You said *Drummond?*"

Kaufman looked confused. "Pardon?"

"Drummond DeLuna claimed materials went missing?"

"Yes. Drummond DeLuna, primary partner at CDE. He hired you for a security check and now—"

I shook my head. "Carlos DeLuna hired me. I've never met Drummond. Perhaps they're working together, but Drummond's name was not on the contract."

Kaufman turned to Anderson. Anderson bent to Kaufman. They conferred.

I waited.

Kaufman looked unhappy. He said, "If you'll give us a moment," and the two men stepped out into the cramped hallway.

Wheels spun different directions in my head, like gears in a transmission trying to mesh but the cogs not lining up. It might be a good thing that I'd been duped by Drummond. That pointed the deception and suspicion away from me. Or it was a bad thing and drew me in deeper. And I still didn't know if there was exposure for J'Leah. Gears slipping, looking for purchase.

Kaufman and Anderson made calls in the hallway. I couldn't make out much of what was said. I got the gist that they were unhappy. Then my mind wandered to wondering if they were using the pedestrian airwaves. If their confidential FBI calls rode on the same signal as me and everyone else, or if they had a special satellite signal or wavelength. Secret fed phones.

The talking stopped and Kaufman re-entered my office and sat in the chair. Anderson resumed his position in the doorway. They didn't bother to tell me if their phones were secure or not. I guess I didn't need to know.

Kaufman pinned his shoulders back. "It's not possible that you met with Carlos DeLuna. He's been in Mexico City for the past three weeks with his wife, who is getting treatment for cancer at the *Instituto Nacional de Cancerologia*." He pronounced it like a pro.

I tried to hide it, but most people have a tell when they're confused. I was no exception. I felt the surprise on my face all the way down into my bones.

"Mister Flint?"

"Hang on a second. Carlos is in Mexico City?"

Kaufman pursed his lips. "With his wife Judy."

"But he was at the restaurant last night."

"Drummond DeLuna—"

"Carlos drives the Ghibli. I followed him to his house—to a property owned by Carlos DeLuna, not Drummond. I looked up the property records."

Kaufman took a little pad of paper from his jacket pocket and wrote something on it. He held the pad up to Anderson and pointed at something he'd written.

Anderson tapped on his phone and retreated a step back into the hallway.

Kaufman penciled another item onto his notepad, then rose and stood in the doorway with Anderson. They consulted again.

I waited again.

Then Kaufman and Anderson came back to their respective plac-es, as if they'd been given assigned seating. Or standing, in the case of Anderson. Kaufman read an address from his pad.

I nodded. "That's the home address for Carlos. Where I followed him—the car—where I…"

Kaufman read the registration for the plates on the Ghibli.

I sighed. I'd been looking at those all week. "That's the vehicle."

Anderson seemed to be enjoying my discomfort. He smirked from the doorway. "You need a minute? Mister P.I.?"

Maybe I deserved that, but I wasn't going to answer. I looked at Kaufman. "That was Drummond?"

"Apparently. As I said, Carlos has been in Mexico. We are certain of that."

It didn't make sense. "Drummond was driving a car registered to his brother, *and* living in Carlos' house?"

Kaufman seemed sympathetic. "It appears so. At least temporarily. As cover, perhaps. I can see how normally your work to search the prop-erty records would have been due diligence for the situation."

"Normally."

"And we are correct in thinking that you believed you were hired by Carlos? You never suspected otherwise?"

"That's right." Anderson smirked again. I didn't care. I wondered what that meant for the contract I'd signed. With Carlos' name and Drummond's signature, would that open questions about my entry onto the property? Or about J'Leah's work, if they discovered that?

I slapped the desk. "Aw, damn. They're twins?"

Kaufman craned his neck up to Anderson, who leaned down. They whispered. The men straightened. Kaufman said, "Twins."

Elizabeth. She'd said the brothers looked similar. She could have told me they were twins. Maybe she didn't know? If she did, maybe I'd go push that big rock back across the garden path.

Kaufman pulled my thoughts back. "What brought you to the un-disclosed location in Dayton last night that placed you in the vicinity of Drummond DeLuna?"

"You mean to the Wheat Penny?"

Kaufman smiled. "OK, to the Wheat Penny."

This was why private investigators didn't like coincidences. Now I was at the wrong end of one.

"Were you surveilling Drummond DeLuna in some fashion?"

"Well, I thought it was Carlos. I guess it was Drummond."

"And what were your purposes for surveilling him?"

I didn't like the way it sounded. And I didn't like where it might go. "It's standard operating procedure to do a background check on clients."

Kaufman tapped his notepad against his leg. "I see your training with the county sheriff hasn't entirely left you. But this seems like substantially more than an STO background check."

So we were trading language now. I kept it simple. "It was a security check. I'm a thorough guy."

Anderson snickered. He had a point. How thorough was I if I had the wrong guy?

Kaufman remained all business. "The Bureau is interested in why you thought it worth looking so closely into Drummond's—who you thought was Carlos—into Drummond's activities."

I'm sure they were. I offered a shrug. "Client confidentiality."

Kaufman didn't like it. His voice dropped an octave. "It is more than coincidental that you were at the same restaurant last night as Drummond."

Time to drop the coy. Put some cards on the table. I laced my fingers together. "What is it you want to know?"

"As I said, this is an interview. We endeavor to ascertain the extent of your knowledge and engagement with Drummond DeLuna and CDE Enterprises."

It was mumbo-jumbo. Department-issued language, or something he'd picked up from legal. He wasn't asking anything specific. And that meant they were fishing. They didn't know what they were trying to get from me. I unlaced my fingers and clasped my hands together behind my head. "You know what I was hired for. You know that I performed a physical check of the CDE site. I followed Drummond, who was posing as Carlos, as part of the detail. What else is there?"

Kaufman waited me out.

I mentally ran through the terms of the contract. Neither Kaufman nor Anderson seemed to know J'Leah by name. They hadn't even asked me about the cyber check. Maybe now I could fish. Or at least redirect. "Have you looked into any interest in another party buying the company?"

Both Kaufman and Anderson looked surprised. Kaufman said, "CDE?"

"Or any interest in the brothers selling it?"

More blank looks.

So they didn't know. Or it wasn't true. I wondered if the bit about one of the brothers being a risk was true. Or more cover story. But cover for what, exactly?

Kaufman and Anderson had quieted. I took the opportunity to press. "What projects is CDE working on for the government?"

Kaufman shook his head. "That's classified."

"What government agency?"

"Classified."

"Is it the Air Force?"

Kaufman waved a hand.

"Who—"

He waved again. "It's all classified."

This was going nowhere. I did the thing with my fingers again, slowly, deliberately lacing them together on the desk. "And what would you hope to gain from obtaining a warrant for my personal possessions?"

Kaufman reached to his throat as if there was a tie for him to straighten. But there was no tie. "If we were able to get a warrant, that would be carefully targeted for the parameters of the case."

More mumbo-jumbo. And I'd noticed the change in language. *If* they were able to get a warrant. They'd been hoping I would reveal something. But this thing was such a mess I didn't even know what I could reveal. I picked up my phone. "You gentlemen are familiar with my family?"

Kaufman nodded cautiously. Anderson did nothing. They knew.

"You've done a background check on me." I flicked to photos and pulled up one of Cali from the week before. "You'll recognize this as my daughter Cali?"

Anderson softened. He looked interested. Kaufman looked sincere.

I focused on Kaufman. "You may have children. I don't know." I shifted my gaze to Anderson. "You might also, but I'll bet you've never had a teenaged daughter."

Anderson shook his head no.

I swiped to another photo of Cali and held the phone up so they could see. "My daughter will not be happy if you take her phone and laptop away." I swiped again, to a photo of Cali and me together in a sunflower field. "She may never forgive me if that happens."

They both looked at the photo.

"That might sound overly dramatic, but to my daughter it will feel that way. An invasion of privacy. She knows nothing about my work for DeLuna." I drew the phone back and put my eyes on Kaufman. "How old?"

He knew what I meant. "A daughter and a son. She's sixteen."

"So you know what I mean."

His eyes said I had him.

I said, "Sixteen is a tough age. Sweet, but tough. Especially for a daughter. It's just Cali and me. We lost her mother almost two years ago now. You would know that. It makes things harder."

Anderson was looking human. I glanced at him. "You have children?"

He didn't want to answer. Then he slowly raised two fingers. "Daughters."

Uh-huh. "A warrant would be hard on Cali. I think you know that. Is there some way I can help the Bureau that might be a little easier on everyone?"

Kaufman cleared his throat. "A warrant may still be forthcoming, but..." He readjusted himself on the chair, avoiding the look he was getting from Anderson. "If you would prepare for us a report of your activities relating to your employment with CDE, including any materials, photos, documents, or other observations."

"That's usually confidential."

Kaufman extracted a business card from his breast pocket. It was one of my cards. Where he'd gotten it, I didn't know. He held the card out between two fingers. "As you say, this does indicate that you are discreet."

I waited.

"But I hope in this case you might see the prudence of making an exception. I don't think Drummond will be in much of a position to make a complaint."

I didn't know if their threat of a warrant had been overplayed, or if they were just parrying. Whatever, I'd take the opening. Breaking client confidentiality privilege with Drummond, who wasn't Carlos, wasn't going to be a stretch for me.

Kaufman had his phone in hand. "We should exchange numbers."

We did that. His prefix was local. Nothing special. No secret fed number, no private extension, no secure spy phone. Kaufman had an android, and it didn't look new. I was a little disappointed.

Anderson did not share his number. It was clear he wasn't the boss.

Then Kaufman rose. "Expect that you'll hear from us again. If we are successful in retrieving the necessary items from the CDE work, this shouldn't become an undue amount of trouble for you. There may have to be some limited procurement of personal items."

I wanted to feel relieved about two things: Cali and J'Leah. They might not take Cali's things. And they didn't seem to know who J'Leah was, or that there were some files that had been copied and locked away.

But when the feds come knocking on your door, it's hard to feel good about much of anything.

18

THE DAY HAD DARKENED. The men in black suits and shiny shoes had done it. That sounds like a metaphor, but it isn't.

The men were gone. My office was as empty as if they'd never been there. The folding chair was closed up and leaned back against the wall. The room was silent. The door hung open just a touch into the hallway, the only visible clue that anyone had been there at all.

My desk was clear and empty. The room smelled of coffee from the pot on top of the filing cabinet. The men had not left scent nor scrap that they'd been there. But the day had changed. Thoreau said that the highest of arts was to affect the quality of the day. He meant to elevate the day. My visitors had affected the opposite. They'd diminished the quality of the day.

I supposed they'd had to. It was their job. The FBI's mission is to protect the American people and uphold the Constitution of the United States. I knew the motto: Fidelity, Bravery, and Integrity. I'd rubbed shoulders with the FBI when I worked for the county Sheriff. They were good for their word. But it had still diminished my day.

I guessed I'd done my own share of diminishing others' days in the course of my job. That didn't make me feel any better.

I looked out my window. The sun had retreated behind a raft of graying clouds. The clouds were thick but not yet ominous. My mood said they would become more ominous. How quickly things change.

There was a sprinkling of people on the street. Clouds were keeping the crowds away. I twisted my neck and looked farther up and down the avenue.

Black paint and gold stripes winked at me from a vehicle at the curb. The Brickmobile. The shiny GT-350, with the top down. Very manly for this fall weather.

I picked up my jacket. Maybe Brick could provide some perspective. I hadn't decided what to tell J'Leah about the feds. Or Cali, if they came for her phone and laptop. I thought on the way down to the street that it's a distinctly human thing to bring your burdens to your friends. But that's exactly what we did, and I was going to take mine to Brick.

The Saturday village vibe was there even under the clouds. There were caffeinators and breakfast-goers, a busker, bench-sitters, pooch-walkers, and conversation. I waded through it to the Shelby to look for the big man.

The first few drops of rain reached my nose, then retreated, a tease for what was coming. I passed Dark Star Books and found Brick standing in front of Glen Garden Gifts flower shop, looking in through the display windows.

I stuck my head up next to his and looked in the window too. "Lose somebody in there?"

He kept looking and didn't say anything. I'd never seen Brick with flowers, buying flowers, thinking about flowers, or talking about them.

I tried something else. "Top's down on the Shelby."

"Yeah."

I held a hand up as if to check for rain. "Gonna get wet."

He stayed looking in the window. "Screw it."

Screw it? That car was Brick's baby. He'd been restoring it for more than a year. Screw it?

Another scattering of raindrops fell. I tugged a ballcap out of my pocket and onto my head. "Something bothering you?"

"You could say."

That was it. Nothing more to tell. He kept looking in the window.

I turned away.

Brick shuffled his feet. "Don't worry. Nobody died."

"Well, now I'm worried. Is someone sick?"

"No. Angelita says I've been grumpy."

"Angelita Rojas Flores?"

"The one."

I pointed in the flower shop window. "Get her something red."

He frowned.

"Rojas flores. Red flowers."

"I get it." His frown deepened.

"Maybe she's right. Have you been grumpy?"

His look already told me, but Brick owned up to it. "You could say so."

Apparently Angelita had said so. "You think flowers are going to fix that?"

"Women like flowers. Is that right?"

"Near as I can tell."

"So I'm looking for flowers for her."

"Sure. Be easier if you went inside."

He grunted. More raindrops sprinkled down.

I said, "Maybe flowers aren't the whole solution."

A single fat raindrop fell onto Brick's forehead. He wiped it away and started across the street for the Shelby.

I followed, and we raised the top and secured it.

Brick took a towel from the trunk and wiped the seats where they'd been dappled by the drops. Then he got into the driver's seat.

I leaned into the passenger window. "So no flowers?"

"Like you say, maybe that's not the answer."

"Flowers for you then?"

He didn't smile.

I tried again. "Make you less grumpy."

He reached over and pushed the passenger door open. "Jackson, get in."

"Huh?"

"Get in the car."

"OK."

"I need to go hit something. You're coming with me."

I got in. "If it'll make you happy. As long as it's not me you're going to hit."

He turned the car around and headed out of the village.

I wiped fog from my window. "I assume you have something specific in mind?"

"Bag."

The heavy bag in Brick's barn. It'd been a while since we'd worked it. Or what was left of the bag after Brick had been pummeling it for the past several years.

We cleared the little business district and Brick stepped on the gas and opened up the Shelby's jets. Over the roar, he said, "Quando's gone."

I stayed quiet and gave him room to tell it at his own pace.

"Just walked away. Four days now."

"Four days?"

"You remember when I was looking for him?"

I did. I tried to count the days backward. "You haven't heard anything?"

"No texts. No calls. Nothing. I've been trying all week."

"And you're just now telling me?"

A hard look came into Brick's eye. You took your burdens to your friends. Why hadn't he done that with me?

He clicked the wipers once. "What were you going to do?"

"We'll find him."

Brick shifted. "You probably could. Not sure what that would do."

My neck tensed. "What do you mean, what would that do? Maybe the kid's in trouble."

Brick knew what I meant. "You're thinking maybe he went back to his crew."

I was. Quando had been in a bad place when he stepped away from his boys and into Brick's old Jeep. I thought that had meant something. But change takes time. The old world pulls on you.

Brick twisted his grip on the wheel. "That's what I'm thinking too."

"That would make it easier. We could find them. Might take some time, but we'd find them."

He stared straight ahead. "Yeah."

A moment passed. "Well?"

"Might not be a good idea."

I sat on that for a minute. "You're gonna have to explain that one to me."

Brick let out a really long breath. "I don't think he wants to come back. If he did, he would have tried that by now."

He had a faraway look that I recognized. I'd seen it on him when he talked about his brother who disappeared into the gang life when Brick was young. I looked out the window at the clouds. "You're sure he ran off? Maybe it could be something else?"

"He took his stuff."

"All of it?"

"There wasn't much. Just some stuff I bought him."

That made sense. Quando had come away with Brick with nothing but the clothes on his back. "Still could be something else. Maybe his old crew found him."

"No. He left. I know it."

"You want to tell me how?"

"Video doorbell."

"You have a video doorbell?"

"Yeah." He drove.

"And?"

"I saw him leave. He had his things. Just walked out and closed the door behind him. No one else there."

My voice got louder. "And you're just now telling me this?"

Brick's shoulders hunched. "I just looked at the video."

I couldn't believe it. "When?"

"Today."

I sat back. "Have you told Angelita?"

"No."

"Well that's the first thing you should do."

"I was going to tell her today. That's why I was looking for flowers."

It made sense, in a weird way. "Then let's go back to the flower shop."

Brick shook his head. "Nope. Now we're going to hit the bag."

We turned onto the last stretch of road before Brick's cabin. I said, "This doesn't make sense. I thought he wanted to stay. You were going to talk to the lawyer. And Marzi."

"Yup."

But Quando didn't stay. I'd gone to Brick to laden him with my burdens, and now instead he'd dropped his on me. That's the way it went sometimes. I breathed. "You think maybe he went back to his mother?"

"Maybe. Does that make a difference?"

I guessed not.

We reached the narrow lane that cut through the trees to Brick's cabin. He nosed the Shelby between the honeysuckle and scrub trees and crossed into the tunnel of walnut and black cherry and oak that led to the cabin.

We rolled past the homestead, and Brick nosed the Shelby up to the barn. I jumped out and opened the doors. He pulled in.

Then Brick got out the boxing gloves and tugged them on. He moved like a cloud of energy, dark and brooding. I squared myself behind the bag to hold it.

Brick unloaded a left. The bag jumped, and me behind it. He unloaded a left-right, and the bag popped.

I moved as Brick moved, circling to stay behind the bag from him. He exploded another hard combination, then slowed to more tactical strikes. I backed away from the bag and let him go into a long series of right-left-something-something-something.

After about five minutes, the steam just went out of him. He dropped his hands and looked at his shoes. "You want to hit some?" He peeled off one glove and then the other and held them out to me.

I took the gloves and set them on the weight bench.

Brick kicked at dust on the floor. "He could have at least told me."

I sat on the bench.

Brick paced. "What did I do wrong?"

I didn't want to pretend I had an answer to give, but I offered something up. "Might not have been entirely just about you."

He went to the cupboard and pulled down a jug of water and took a long drink. When he came back, Brick leaned against a barn post. "Sorry."

"Nothing to be sorry for."

He drank some more. "You don't want to hit the bag?"

"No."

He looked at me. "I take you away from something?"

"Nah."

We were quiet for a minute. Dust motes floated through the air. Brick set the jug of water down. "I'll be all right."

"Of course you will."

More dust floated through the quiet.

"You want me to take you back?"

"Eh."

"What then? It's going to rain. Probably can't climb the barn."

"Nah, I guess you should take me back."

He stared at me. "You got something you want to say?"

"No."

"It's OK, you want to say it."

I held up a hand. "No. I got nothing helpful to say about Quando. I wish I did. If there's something you want me to do, just tell me." I got up and walked to the Shelby.

Brick's eyes followed me. "What is it?"

"Nothing." I got in the car and waited.

Brick came to the driver's side and leaned on the top, looking in.

I reached over and rolled down the window. "What?"

"Say it."

I put both hands up.

"You got something to say about Quando."

I sighed. "No. Listen. Get in."

He didn't.

"I was going to ask you about something, but you're having a bad day."

Brick poked his head in through the window. "So tell me. I could use a distraction."

We sat in the Shelby, in the barn, and I told him about Drummond DeLuna and CDE and what had happened. Then I told him about the feds.

He got antsy. "That is…"

"I know."

Brick shadow boxed a couple of feints in the seat of the Shelby. There wasn't much room for it. "What else?"

I filled in some details about trailing Drummond. I told him the feds might get a warrant.

"They're going to look through your things?"

"Maybe. And maybe Cali's."

His head went back and forth. "She's not going to like that."

"You're telling me."

He juked his head and balled his fists again. "If we could just find this guy."

"I was hoping you could give me some advice about what to tell J'Leah."

He stopped juking. "J'Leah?"

I filled him in about what J'Leah had done and the copied files.

He didn't like it. "That whole thing stinks."

"It does."

"DeLuna set you up."

"Maybe. But for what?"

"Throw the feds off the trail."

I shrugged. "Feds are on to DeLuna. They were fishing with me."

"Maybe he's setting up J'Leah."

"Again, I'd like to know what for. DeLuna doesn't know her name. The feds don't seem to know about her at all."

"You're missing something."

I threw my hands up. "You think?"

"If we could find this guy, we could make him talk."

"Oh, I can find him."

Brick's head snapped over. "What?"

"I can find him. That's not the problem."

"Then what's the problem?"

"What am I going to do? Shake the answers out of him?'

Brick made two fists. "Exactly."

I ran my hands through my hair. If only it was that easy.

Brick fidgeted. "How do we find him?"

"What?"

"DeLuna. You said you could find him. How?"

This was starting to feel like a really bad idea.

"How?"

I shrugged.

Brick put out a hand. "Give me your phone."

"I don't think that's a good idea."

The hand stayed there. "Your phone."

I took my phone from my pocket.

Brick plucked it from my hand.

"Now wait a minute." I reached to take the phone back.

Brick blocked me. "You've still got the tracker on him."

"I don't think that's helpful."

"The feds are going to find him."

"They probably already have."

Brick had my phone unlocked. Did everybody know how to do that? He swiped for the apps. "Maybe we can find him first."

I reached for my phone again. "And do what?"

"Get some answers."

"Like I said, the FBI will do that."

"We can do it faster. And better for you and J'Leah."

I pressed my palms into my eye sockets. "Look, this isn't going to help. I told you—"

"Somebody's going to get whooped."

My palms came down. "What?"

"I can't do anything about Quando." His words were a jumble. "But I can damn sure do something about this DeLuna guy."

"Brick…"

He started the Shelby. "Get the barn door."

I stayed in my seat.

Brick opened his door and stepped out.

"Wait." I got out. "I'll get it."

Brick climbed back into the Shelby.

I stuck my head back in. "We'll just go have a look. A talk if we find him. Nothing else. Right?"

Brick pointed to the barn door.

It was a bad idea. To affect the quality of the day. Thoreau had been a wise man. He wanted us to elevate the quality of our day.

It was probably too late for that now.

19

BRICK POINTED US WEST, toward the Air Force base. My phone rested in the console above the stick shift. The tracker pushed us steadily toward Drummond's office. It was the first time it struck me as odd that DeLuna had an office away from the CDE compound. Sure, the action was near the base, but the brothers had gone to some trouble to build and secure the fortress in the fields. It was just one more thing to wonder about with the DeLunas.

We reached the highway bypass and Brick maneuvered toward the ramp. The rain had fizzled. A spattering of mist rose from the tires and dusted the windows.

I raised my voice above the engine as Brick accelerated down the ramp. "So this is a bad idea, right?"

Brick pushed the Shelby faster. "Probably."

"Maybe we'll change our minds before we get there."

"Maybe."

We passed the old quarry sites and the cement tower that loomed in the distance. I watched them recede behind us and said, "The feds could be there."

"That might change our minds for us."

It would. "What do you think we'll accomplish if we find Drummond?"

Brick held the Shelby at seventy. It was a smooth ride for an old sports car. We hugged the slippery road without so much as a tick in the wheel. "He'll tell us what's really going on."

"What if it's nothing?"

"The feds don't come for nothing. What if it's DeLuna setting you up for stealing a secret government project?"

What if it was. "That's what it looks like, but I don't think he can make it stick. The guys who showed up at my office couldn't even get a warrant."

We passed under the long pedestrian bridge and the first of the big white buildings that housed businesses that either served the government's needs or siphoned money from the federal till, or both. That reminded me why DeLuna had an office here. Follow the money.

The buildings went by and I squinted at the names on them. Then I looked over at Brick. "Are we really doing this because of Quando?"

Brick stared ahead. "We're doing this because this guy has screwed you. That ain't right."

"Neither is Quando running off."

He stared at the road some more.

I added, "Without a word."

Now Brick looked over. "Who does that?"

"I guess you were getting used to having him around."

"And I guess I'm going to have to get *un*used to it. We were going to get Samuel Thomas to look into me getting custody."

"Quando wanted that?"

"Said he did."

"That's a long-term thing."

"Kid's fifteen. It would have been at least a few years."

He'd thought it through. Some. "Raising a kid, even part of the time, is more long-term than that. Lasts a lifetime if you do it right."

Our exit neared. Brick moved into the ramp lane. "Not anymore. Kid's gone."

He was back to using *the kid*. Not Quando anymore, just some kid who was there and now he wasn't. It didn't feel right. My eyes slid to the glovebox. "You have the Glock?"

"No."

It was unusual. And for the best. I didn't point that out.

Brick made a turn and followed the dot on the phone.

I pointed to an entry to the parking lot. "There. You want to play good cop, bad cop?"

He turned again. "We're not cops."

I was acutely aware of that. I'd been a cop, and interviews and interrogations had been carefully monitored. "You sure I can't talk you out of this?"

It was Saturday. Not many cars in the lot, but the Ghibli was there. Brick circled once and took a spot pointed at the exit. He opened his door and started for the building. "Sure you can."

I followed. It didn't look like I could talk him out of it. Instead, I worked on my game face. This still felt like it was more for Brick than for me. But if we were going to play it, I wanted some mileage. Get something for it.

The place seemed empty. People had better things to do on their weekend. Like when I'd been there before, the doors didn't have security. I hadn't paid attention to other details the last time. I did now.

I caught up to Brick at the door and put a hand in front of his nose, then pointed to a camera mounted on the outside wall.

He slowed. "Too late for that." But he tipped his head down. It wouldn't do much to hide us if things went really sour.

Inside the door, another camera tilted toward the hallway and the elevator. We moved away from that and took the stairs.

I didn't see any cameras in the stairway. It didn't mean they weren't there.

We went up to the third floor. Brick stood beside the stairway door, pushed it open with his fingertips, and peered around.

I walked past him into the hallway. "Too late for that."

No doors were open on our end of the hall. A fish-eyed turret with a gray lens winked from a perch on the ceiling. There were no sounds, not even the mechanical hum or whisper of HVAC. 'Twas the night before Christmas. We were the mice.

We walked the hall and passed beneath the camera turret with our heads down.

Drummond's door was halfway open. Lucky us. The door opened directly into Drummond's—or maybe Carlos'—office. He stood in front of the desk with his back to us, looking at something in a cardboard packing box. There were no men in black suits or anyone else in the room with him.

Brick pushed the door wide open and leaned against the frame, cool as a turtle in mud.

I stepped past Brick into the room.

Drummond turned. He looked like he'd been caught necking under the bleachers. "Uhm…"

I stepped closer.

He said, "Mister Flint."

"Yes."

"And…?" Drummond's eyes went to Brick.

"My associate."

Drummond's embarrassed look faded to confused. "I thought we had concluded our business."

"Not quite."

"Oh, ah, did the uh, check clear?"

"It did."

He stepped back, inching toward the far end of the desk. "As I said, the report isn't necessary. What you've done is sufficient."

I stuck my hand out.

Drummond looked from me to my hand to Brick leaning against the door and back to me. "Of course." He found a weak little smile that barely stuck to his face and he reached out, the old glad-hander. "You'd like to complete the business in person." Then he foolishly took my hand. Who shakes nicely with someone who has just fired him?

I squeezed. "Precisely. *Drummond.*"

The precarious smile on his face slipped away.

"Perhaps I should give my report to your brother Carlos and his wife in Mexico City."

Drummond tried to pull away. "You probably think…"

I held onto his hand. "I do. You lied to me."

He tried to shake his head, but it was coming out wrong. "There's been a mistake."

"There has. Two gentlemen in black suits came to visit me this morn-ing. You need to tell me why."

"Can you please just—let go of my hand."

I did.

He massaged his fingers and palm.

I didn't give him a chance to get comfortable. "Drummond. Why did the FBI come to my office this morning?"

He stepped back. "That's a question I can't answer."

I matched his step. "You don't understand. I'm not *asking* you to tell me why you lied. I'm *telling* you." I ticked an eye toward Brick. "My as-sociate would also like to know."

"You can't just..." Drummond reached the end of his desk and squirmed around behind it.

I let him.

He pulled his phone from his pocket and touched the screen.

I put a finger in front of his nose. "I've been very nice. You haven't. You can put that phone down, or I'll do it for you."

Drummond's eyes went to the door. It was filled with Brick. "Are you going to hurt me?"

"Why would I want to hurt you?"

Drummond lowered his phone.

I kept my finger to his nose. "You've put my daughter at risk. And my friends. That makes me very unhappy. Tell me why the FBI is at my door. Tell me why you lied to me."

His head shook in short, quick strokes. "I don't know."

"You do know. And I need to know. To protect myself. This isn't difficult."

Drummond pushed my finger away from his face, scrambled out around the other end of the desk, and dove for the door. He aimed low for the gap between Brick's knees and the jamb.

There wasn't enough room. It didn't matter. Brick stepped forward, closed the door behind him, and put out a knee.

Drummond hit Brick, then Drummond hit the carpet.

Brick reached down and got hold of the back of Drummond's belt and shirt collar and lifted. Drummond came up dangling like a crab, arms milling for purchase he wouldn't find. A button popped on the front of his shirt as his body sagged against his clothes. Then Brick tilted Drummond upright. "You seem to have fallen. I'm just helping you up."

Drummond stumbled to gain his feet.

Brick looked my way. "You suck at good cop." He pointed at Drummond. "You tell the man what he wants to know or we're going to do this another way."

Drummond tried to step around Brick and reach the closed door.

Brick frowned and lifted Drummond by the armpits. "That—" He wrapped one arm around Drummond and under his arms and pushed the other into Drummond's ribs. "Is enough." He ripped the door open and carried Drummond out into the hallway.

I followed. Brick moved fast. They passed under the camera turret in what looked like an awkward dance. At least that's what I hoped it would look like if anyone reviewed the feed.

Drummond squealed as Brick pulled him into the stairwell. No office doors had opened. No voices had called out. There were no sounds except the very faint whisper of air from the vents. Still quiet as a church mouse.

I caught them at the top of the stairs. The door to the stairwell closed behind me as Brick was tipping Drummond across the top rail, edging him over empty space below.

Drummond's voice came as a hoarse whisper. "Stop."

Brick pressed Drummond up onto his toes. "The man here has some questions."

I leaned over the rail so Drummond could see me. "First question. Easy. Why did you tell me you were Carlos?"

"I didn't…"

I didn't wait long. "Next question. Why did you hire me? You didn't want a security check."

"I—it's complicated."

"You don't want to sell CDE."

Drummond wheezed. "No."

"What did you use me for?"

Drummond shook his head.

Brick lifted Drummond higher onto his toes and over the rail.

That did it. Drummond said, "My brother, he wants to steal from me. He needs the money. For his wife who is ill."

"I've heard this story before. But you were the other brother then."

Drummond struggled against Brick. It was no use. "Carlos, he wanted to take the—Please mister, let me up. I will talk to you, I will tell."

Brick kept Drummond at the rail but let him take some air.

"There is a project. For the company. It is very lucrative." Drummond's feet scrabbled as they found better contact with the floor.

I rolled a finger. Don't get comfortable. Go on.

"This is maybe why the men came to you today."

"I'm aware of that. What's the project? What's happening with it that the FBI are talking to me?"

"That's classified."

I sighed and stepped back. "This is bad."

Brick lifted Drummond by his belt.

Drummond coughed and struggled. "You would not let me fall."

I leaned to his ear again. "You could fall on your own. Distressed. It happens."

"You would learn nothing."

"I'm learning nothing now." I stepped away. This is where someone had to blink. We weren't going to drop him. If Drummond called our bluff, it was game over. Brick's move.

Without a word, Brick hoisted Drummond by the ankles, pushed him over the rail, and held him upside down over the drop.

Drummond grabbed wildly for something to hold onto. Brick's arms swayed with the movement. The grabbing stopped, and the swaying slowed. Drummond squeaked. "Batteries!"

"Batteries?"

Drummond's cell phone slipped from his pocket, plinked against a stair, and bounced down three floors to the bottom.

"I'll talk! I'll tell you. Pull me back!"

Brick lifted Drummond with practiced precision and pulled him back over the rail.

Drummond bent onto his knees and breathed. "Batteries are the future. And the materials to make them. Metals, raw materials. My brother is a genius with small things. Electrical circuits, conductivity. He is making batteries that are smaller, better. With materials that are plentiful." The words came out as if Drummond was spitting out something that tasted bad. His breath was short.

I pressed him. "Plentiful?"

"New materials. Cheap. New cheap batteries."

"Why would that be a secret?"

"Everyone wants batteries from materials that are easy to get."

"And?"

Drummond straightened a little and settled his breath. "Carlos also builds a guidance system, with drones that are run by these little batteries and can recharge themselves."

"Rechargeable batteries? That's not new."

"They recharge in flight."

"In flight?"

A nod. "Without humans. The supply drone flies up, attaches to a surveillance drone—or an ordinance drone, and recharges the other."

That sounded new. "These things can endlessly recharge and keep flying?"

Drummond nodded. "This is just the start of it."

I looked at Brick for his take. He rolled a finger. Keep going. He was buying it.

I leaned into Drummond again. "Where do I come in? Why hire me?"

Drummond eyed me sideways. "Carlos. He wants to steal the designs. Take them for himself. He would leave the company with nothing." Drummond looked pleased to have revealed it.

I didn't like it. He was too confident. "And?"

"I planned to steal the work before Carlos could."

I touched the top of the rail and looked down. "It doesn't fit. Where do I come in?"

"You were cover. You stole the materials. Then I could take them and…" Drummond spread his hands in a sloppy I'm sorry gesture.

I looked at Brick.

Brick didn't like it either.

I looked back to Drummond. "That's stupid."

He shrugged and grinned. The grin did it. Brick bent and grabbed Drummond by the ankles again.

Drummond shrieked. "No! There—it doesn't work!"

Brick hesitated.

Drummond collapsed. "It's fake. All of it. None of it works. It never will."

Brick let go of Drummond.

My head hurt. "You were going to set me up for…what, exactly?"

"The material had to be stolen. It was altered. Falsified. I couldn't let that be discovered. The contracts are worth a lot of money. I didn't want to lose them."

"So you—" It was too absurd to put together. "That was never going to work. No one will believe—whatever you were trying to sell."

Drummond looked like he might cry. "I understand that now." Then he did blubber, softly, indiscriminately, embarrassingly. "I was desperate."

I gave Brick the high sign. Wind it up. Let's go.

He nodded and started down the stairs. I followed.

Drummond called down after us. "I can make it up to you, my friend. I will make it right." Always the salesman. Brassing it out to the end.

Brick and I descended.

Carlos called again. "Mister Jackson. Mister Jackson."

It was Flint. Mister Flint. We reached the bottom of the stairwell and stepped over the shattered bits of Drummond's cell phone. Brick bent and picked up a quarter that had dropped from Drummond's pocket and flipped it into the air like a lucky coin and caught it. Mister cool. Like he hung guys out over the stairs by their ankles every day.

Back in the Shelby, Brick flicked the defrost on to clear the windshield.

I wiped a shirtsleeve across my window. "Feel better?"

"Remarkably."

"That was incredibly stupid."

"Remarkably."

"There are a whole bunch of ways that could have gone wrong—still can."

"Agreed." He put the Shelby into gear.

"I can't believe…Who—you could have dropped him."

"Agreed. He was getting wiggly."

I slumped. "This is going to bite us."

"Jackson."

"It is absolutely going to come back and—"

"Jackson?" Brick put a hand on my shoulder.

"What?"

"I think we got away with it."

I didn't. "We'll see."

"Who's he going to tell?"

I held up a hand with my fingers extended and pushed one down. "The federal agents." I pushed another finger down. "The local authorities, if it comes to that." I pushed down a third finger. "And…" I dropped my hand. "Your mother."

Brick laughed. "And he's going to tell the agents what?"

"That we assaulted him."

"He fell down. I helped him up."

I frowned as hard as I could at Brick. He navigated across the lot.

The blower whirred. The fog started to clear from the windshield. The world reappeared.

"I suck at good cop?"

We reached the gate and Brick pulled onto the road. "It's OK. You'd stink at bad cop too."

"Thanks."

"Da nada."

This whole thing stunk. It was messy, and I didn't know if we'd made it messier. What good was what we'd learned from Drummond, if he'd even been telling the truth?

I brooded as we rode back to the village. Brick looked over after a few minutes. I looked back. "What?"

"It looks like you're getting over it."

"Maybe. I just had a happy thought."

"What's that?"

"Our new workout. Hanging by the ankles."

He laughed. "You want me to hang you over the hayloft by your ankles?"

"No. I want to hang you."

20

WHEN WE REACHED the highway bypass, Brick said, "You want me to drop you at your office?"

I was looking out the window watching the world go by. The day had gone off the rails. It started terrifically with a run and coffee and pastries and breakfast with Cali. Went downhill with the FBI, and then Brick and Drummond. And now I had to do what might be the hardest part.

"Actually…"

Brick switched lanes and passed an Amazon van. "What?"

"I was going to ask you about how to tell J'Leah."

"Tell her what?"

I lifted a finger. "The feds." I lifted another. "Drummond. Who isn't Carlos." I went back to the first finger. "But mostly about the FBI."

"She's not going to like it."

"That's what I figure."

"You think it changes anything?"

I went back to my fingers. "Which? The FBI or Drummond?"

"Either."

I let the fingers down. "I don't know."

"That's why you've got to call her."

"So no advice then?"

He didn't offer any.

I picked up my phone. "She doesn't really like phone calls."

Brick changed lanes again and found some open ground to put the Shelby into. "So text her."

I did. The message was simple. *There are developments. We need to catch up.* That would give me time to—

My phone rang. "Jackson."

"J'Leah."

"Developments?"

"Are you some place private?"

"Hang on." There was the sound of footsteps, and maybe something being moved. "Now."

"It's not all good."

"Do I need to take notes?"

"Maybe." I told her about the FBI agents in my office.

She listened. "Uh-huh."

I told her that Carlos wasn't Carlos, he was Drummond.

"Uh-huh" again. This time with a little more feeling.

I told her about the visit Brick and I just had with Drummond.

"Uh-huh." That one came with enough feeling that I pulled the phone back a few inches from my ear.

I told her what Drummond had said when Brick held him by the ankles over the stairs.

"What? You two are really stupid, you know that?"

I looked at Brick. He nodded. He'd heard. I said, "You mean specifically the—"

"I mean the whole thing. Holding him over rail?"

"That was Brick."

"Is he there?"

"He is."

"Put him on."

"He's driving. I'll hold the phone up." I raised my arm and—

"That was stupid!"

Brick twitched.

I brought the phone back to my hear. "He heard you. And now that we've gotten that out of our system, can we get back to a few things?"

"What things?"

"How to manage the FBI. If we made the right decision to bury the copied files."

J'Leah breathed. "Or if we should look through all of them again."

"Or turn them over."

"I vote against that." I could almost see her head shaking.

"I do too. The good news is they don't seem to know about you. Or that you copied some files from CDE."

"Who is they?"

"The FBI."

"You're sure?"

"None of them mentioned it. I'm assuming you haven't been visited?"

"I haven't. But now you're making me paranoid."

I checked Brick's reaction. He'd heard. He said, "J'Leah's not the paranoid type."

"I know."

J'Leah came in. "What am I?"

I ignored her question and said, "I wonder if we want to speculate what happens now?"

"I'm all ears."

"Try this: The feds reel in Drummond. They already know what's going on, whether it's what Drummond told us or not. Doesn't matter. The FBI's interest in me is whether I know more than I've told them, and whether I'm any more a risk of a breach or leak. They'll interview me again. I'll tell them the same story. If no one mentions you or comes to you, it'll end with me."

She was quiet.

"J'Leah?"

"Yeah."

"The question for you is whether they'll find you or not."

"I know. It plays differently depending on the odds."

"It does. If they don't find you, we can do nothing. You'll stay clear. But if it's likely they'll uncover you…"

"We need to decide if it's better to come clean before they do."

"I'm sorry."

She let out a long breath again.

I said, "We might want to expedite that data scrub."

"Or forget the whole thing. There's something that bothers me about this."

"I'm not surprised." I held the phone so Brick could hear better. "What is it?"

"Why haven't they pulled in Drummond yet? Why just let him roam free? Letting you two have access to him wasn't the smartest thing."

"That's a good question. I don't know. Oh—" I glanced at Brick. "There's one more thing I didn't tell you. The kid's gone."

"Quando?"

"Yeah."

"What happened?"

I glanced over. "Maybe I'll let Brick tell it."

His eyes stayed on the road. He didn't talk. I guess he didn't want to explain it.

I said, "There are a lot of unknowns here."

J'Leah agreed. "We could game this out some more."

"You want to meet?"

She sighed. "It's Saturday. I might have a social life."

"Sorry. You've got something?"

She sighed again with much more emphasis. "No."

"An hour?"

"Sure. Let's get this over with."

"My office?"

"Does it always have to be your office? We can't even all fit in there."

"You'd rather we meet in the Faraday cage?"

She might have lightened a little at that. "Your office then. Coffee's on you."

That ended the call.

We glided into the village and back to where we'd started, a spot on the street near the flower shop. It was well after lunch. We were right in front of Current Cuisine. We took that as a sign and went in for sandwiches and came out with curried tofu, black bean enchiladas, broccoli salad, and spinach squares. On the walk up to my office, Brick handed me the tofu and took the enchiladas.

I actually got to sit behind my desk, and I started coffee in the percolator on top of the filing cabinet.

Brick sat on a folding chair and watched. "Saving a few pennies on the coffee?"

It made me think of the wheat penny Quando had found, and that made me think of Quando. You look for satisfaction or happiness wherever you can find it, even if it's just a little slice, like a penny. "College fund. Every penny counts."

Brick spread the food out on my desk. "You're thinking about college already?"

"Are you kidding? Cali graduates next year. I'm about ten years late starting on a college fund."

Brick had a funny look and didn't jump into the enchiladas. Maybe thinking about Quando, like I was.

The percolator gurgled and coffee bubbled up into the little glass globe on top. I opened a drawer on the filing cabinet and took out two cups.

Brick pulled a cup toward him. "That filing cabinet good for anything besides making coffee?"

I pulled the top drawer open. "Water and coffee." I closed that and opened another drawer. "Peanuts, raisins, crackers." I picked up a stained paper bag, looked inside, and reclosed the bag. "Maybe a bagel?"

I opened the bottom drawer. "Razor blade, hat, long-sleeve shirt, change of shoes, sunglasses."

"Razor blade?"

I shrugged. "Came with the cabinet."

"Where did the filing cabinet come from?"

"Came with the office."

"That's kind of gross."

I held up the razor. It was still in its package. "P.I.'s secret weapon. If I need a disguise I can shave. No one would recognize me."

"You think that's funny, but a shave might do you some good." Then Brick found his appetite and started in on the food.

I texted Cali. *Running late.*

Her reply came right away. *How late?*

Uncertain. I'll check back later.

Don't do the magic eight ball. How late?

Cali knew what a magic eight ball was? *Could be a while.*

I'll make plans with Marzi. That was it. Over and out, daddy-O.

When Cali was little she'd wanted her mother's approval or mine constantly. Not now. I knew that was a part of her growing up, but every once in a while I wanted that little girl again who looked up at me like I had all the answers.

The percolator had stopped gurgling. Brick and I ate and drank coffee and waited for J'Leah.

It took her longer to get there than she'd thought. By the time J'Leah arrived, Brick and I had knocked back a lot of food and coffee. We hadn't accomplished much else. The risks of exposure centered on J'Leah. We'd waited to see how she wanted to play it.

J'Leah came around the office door and slipped the backpack off her shoulders. She looked at me. "Unfold another chair for me, will you?"

It was the least I could do. I got up and opened a chair.

J'Leah took the opportunity to slide around me and take the seat behind my desk.

I admitted defeat and folded myself in next to Brick.

J'Leah moved things aside and set her backpack on my desk.

"Comfortable?"

"It'll do." She stacked empty paper food boats. "Are you guys always eating?"

Brick took the bait. "Is that what it looks like to you?"

"Yes."

"Then I guess so."

I pointed to the filing cabinet. "Something there for you, if you want it, and coffee."

She poured half a cup of coffee and didn't look at the food. "You guys ready to get serious?"

Brick frowned. "It's already been a very serious day."

We all looked at each other. Nobody said anything.

J'Leah took a sip of coffee. "Did I tell you guys what you did with Drummond was really stupid?"

Brick adjusted himself on the chair, trying to make more room for his legs. "You mentioned it."

"You left your fingerprints, literally and figuratively, all over that place."

Brick said, "I know."

"There is no reason for that level of sloppiness."

"I know."

"If you'd stopped for a minute—"

"I *know*. I was distracted."

I inserted myself. "Maybe it would help if...Brick told you about Quando."

J'Leah set her cup down and looked at him.

Brick wiggled in his chair. "The boy run off."

"That's it?"

He shrugged. "Then Jackson and I blew off some steam."

J'Leah repeated herself. "That's it? He runs off, and so you go out and—"

I stepped in again. "Look, we know everything that happened wasn't the best choice. But it's done. The feds are going to clean up the DeLuna case. I'm mixed up in it, and now maybe Brick. What we need to decide—" I pointed to J'Leah. "Is what to do about you. No one seems to have put a finger on you. Do you keep your head down and hope they don't find you, or should we be proactive here?"

Brick bent forward. "We keep her out of it. We protect J'Leah."

J'Leah hunched her shoulders. "You don't have to protect me."

Brick leaned on the desk. "Yes, we do. That's how this works."

They locked like that for a second, then Brick broke it. "We protect you. That's not a question. Shred everything, say nothing, and wait. You didn't do anything wrong."

J'Leah said, "I may be unknowingly in possession of something the FBI is going to want."

"Shred everything."

"That will take some time."

"Shred it."

"I'm going to need my security clearance. I can't jeopardize that. We don't know how this is going to play out."

Brick looked at me. "Why are we still talking about this?"

I spread my hands. "J'Leah?"

She stared at us for a long time before she answered. "Shred it."

I ran some fingers through my hair. "I guess you didn't need to come all the way out here for us to decide that."

"I just didn't want you guys to tell me what to do."

I started cleaning up napkins and food wrappers. "Like we could. You all happy with this?"

It seemed we'd made the decision, but no one really seemed happy about it. Then my phone buzzed. I looked at the screen. "Kaufman."

Brick and J'Leah both got quiet, and I squeezed around Brick into the hall. "Jackson Flint."

"I know it's Flint. Where is he?"

I didn't have to pretend to be confused. "He who?"

"He *Drummond*. Where is Drummond DeLuna?"

Brick and J'Leah were leaning in. I tipped the phone out for them to hear better. "Why are you asking me?"

"You were with him."

I didn't comment.

Kaufman did. "At his office."

"Uh-huh?"

"Don't play dumb with me. You saw Drummond today, and now he's gone."

"Gone?"

Now Kaufman didn't answer.

"You lost your man?"

"We haven't lost him. He's on the move. What was the nature of your visit with Drummond?" Muffled voices came over the connection. Kaufman appeared to speak with one of them. None of the words were clear. He came back. "You were accompanied by an unidentified man. Black, over six feet. Driving a...some sort of old sports car."

So Kaufman wasn't an enthusiast.

"They're saying he's big. Muscular."

Brick and I exchanged a look. He wouldn't be unidentified for long.

"Darnell Brickman."

And just like that, they had Brick. "You were watching me?"

"You and Brickman went to see Drummond, then he disappeared. What transpired during your interaction with him?" Even when he was excited, Kaufman sounded like he'd talked to too many lawyers.

I countered. "Why haven't you brought Drummond in?"

"Jackson…"

"Would have kept you from losing him."

Kaufman got louder. "That is agency business. What was the nature of your conversation with Drummond?"

J'Leah was holding up her phone. On the notepad app she'd typed *Drummond more valuable moving around. Looking for something.*

I nodded. "Until they lost him."

Kaufman shouted. "What?"

"Not a thing."

Kaufman's volume went up another notch. "I can have agents sent your way in—right now!"

I looked at Brick and J'Leah. Brick shrugged. J'Leah said, "Tell him."

I did. "Drummond said the project was fake. It didn't work."

The connection went silent.

"Kaufman?"

"You believe him?"

"We were persuasive when we asked."

A beat passed. Kaufman's voice remodulated itself. "Why would Drummond tell you that?"

He didn't question if it was true. He only asked why Drummond would say it. I told him. "I knew Drummond was using me to cover for something. I confronted him about it. He told me he was trying to claim the work was stolen so it wouldn't come out that it didn't work."

Kaufman snorted. "That's stupid."

"That's the conclusion my associate and I came to."

Muffled voices came through the call again. Kaufman said, "Hang on." The muffled voices continued. Then Kaufman came back and said, "I have to advise you not to leave the immediate area. Do not travel or leave the state without first notifying me or someone in the regional of-fice. I'll get that number to you. Your assistance is needed in clearing up a matter of importance to the U.S. government. Your compliance here is subject to…"

Brick made a cutting motion with his hand.

I held the phone away and let Kaufman keep talking. I mouthed, "What?"

Brick whispered. "The tracker. Don't tell them."

It hadn't occurred to me that I would. I gave a thumb up.

Kaufman was still going. I heard, "…convey this same information to your associate Mister Brickman."

A breath passed.

"Jackson?"

"I got it."

"And if Drummond DeLuna contacts you, or you come across anything that may help lead us to him, contact me right away."

"I will."

Kaufman cleared his throat. "This is going to get messier. I hope you'll do what you can to make things easier for you."

"I do too."

The connection broke.

J'Leah waved me closer. "The FBI lost Drummond, but we didn't." She pointed to her phone. "I put the app for the tracker on my phone when I loaded it onto yours."

Of course she had. I shook my head. "I said I wasn't going to look at that anymore. We can let the feds handle this."

She turned her phone around. "You might want to see this. It looks like Drummond is headed right for us."

21

THE LITTLE DOT on the phone traced a route down River Road toward the village of Clifton.

Brick watched the mark. "It's *sort of* coming toward us."

J'Leah laid her phone on the desk. "Where else would he be going?"

"Why would he come here? Jackson and I just saw the man."

I watched the dot. "Brick's right."

The Ghibli passed the last turnoff before River Road ended at the state route. From there, roads went through Clifton, or to Springfield, Cedarville, Xenia, or out in rural directions that could go anywhere.

J'Leah said, "We'll know in a minute."

The Ghibli turned north, then jagged left into the tiny village. That was odd. Clifton was only a few miles away, and it didn't have much in it except the cliffs that the town was named for and an old mill that was a regional sensation for its Christmas lights. The Ghibli took the scenic route past the mill.

We all leaned in. The dot swung through the two blocks of Clifton and turned left. That pointed it right at us.

Brick glanced to the window as if the Ghibli was already there. "Could be coincidence."

I frowned. "I don't like coincidences."

The dot on the map drew closer. J'Leah said, "Feds could be following him. Or tracking him."

I wasn't sure. "They didn't seem to know where he is."

J'Leah said, "The whole thing is weird."

The Ghibli turned onto Route 68. Right toward us.

Brick squeezed around the desk with J'Leah and went to the window. "What do federal vehicles look like?" He unlatched the sash and pushed it up. Cool air swam into the room.

J'Leah clambered around Brick and looked out the window with him. I tried to tip-toe a view over their shoulders.

The Ghibli cruised by right below our noses and kept going.

Brick and J'Leah swung their heads and stared as the car cleared downtown. Then Brick closed the window.

J'Leah was back looking at her phone. "That was anticlimactic."

I rubbed my eyes. "So far."

Brick climbed back around the desk. "Maybe he's turning himself in."

J'Leah was touching her phone. Pinching. Changing the view. "Jackson? You'd better look at this."

I did. The Ghibli turned and cut a path across the village. "Where is he—"

J'Leah caught my eye. She'd already figured it out. The Ghibli turned again. J'Leah said, "That's toward your house."

It was. Cali. Where was Cali? I grabbed my phone and jacket and called as I ran. "Answer. Answer."

She didn't. I ran down the stairs and left a message. "Cali, call me now. If you're in the house, get out. Now. Out the back. I'm coming."

I reached the alley and looped toward the storefronts and the street. I texted Cali. *Answer your phone.*

Brick came up behind and caught my elbow. He pointed up the street to the Shelby. We ran toward it and I called Cali again. It went to message again.

We got in the car and Brick got us out into the street and moving with traffic. The dot on the map slowed and stopped in front of my house.

I called Marzi. She picked up. "Marzi! Is Cali with you? Is she at home?"

"What? Slow down."

"Where is Cali? Is she with you?"

"Why are you shouting?"

"I need to know where Cali is. Is she at home?"

"Jackson, what is going on? I don't like the sound of this."

I almost hung up. Brick was trying to nose the Shelby around cars and find an opening, but we were stuck at the light.

Then Marzi said, "She was supposed to go to Tom's for some things. I'm coming over later."

"Go to Tom's and find her. Don't let her go home. Make sure she doesn't go home."

"I don't—"

"Can you just do that for me?"

"All right." She disconnected.

The Ghibli was still at my house. I pointed to an alley. Brick pulled in. That gave us a route around traffic. Overgrown honeysuckle and branches closed around the car and swept the sides. Brick didn't say a word about the scratches.

We popped out of the alley and Brick turned toward the house. The Ghibli was still there. Brick reached reflectively under his seat. His hand came up empty. The Glock wasn't there.

Two blocks from home, the dot started moving again. One block out, it picked up speed. When we stopped in front of the house, I jumped out and scanned the fields beyond. The Ghibli crested a rise in the road, then dipped back out of sight and disappeared.

Brick had the motor running. "What do you want to do?"

My phone dinged. J'Leah. I put her on speaker.

"He's moving. Where are you guys?"

"The house. He was here. He stopped."

"I saw that."

"He's driving away. We saw the Ghibli."

There was a hum. "I've got visual on him."

The Bolt. She was tracking Drummond on her phone. I almost told J'Leah I loved her. "Anyone with him in the car?"

"I can't tell."

"We can't find Cali. I need to know if she's with him."

"Roger that. I'll get closer."

I ran for the house. The front door was locked. I ran to the back. Unlocked. It was supposed to be locked, but Cali didn't like doing that. Said women's pants weren't made for pockets and keys. If that was our downfall now, I would be inventing a new kind of women's pants.

I yanked the door open and ran inside. "Cali!"

Through the kitchen and living room. "Cali?"

To her room. To my room. She wasn't there.

Brick rumbled in through the kitchen. "She's not outside."

"Damn damn damn."

"We'll find her."

"Yeah."

I spun and ran to my bedroom. I went for the closet and my gun. The closet door was open a few inches. Mrs. Jenkins squatted on the floor and looked in like she was waiting for a mouse to come out.

I dropped to my knees and swept her up with one arm. "Not this time." Conscious be damned, the Smith & Wesson was coming out.

I spun the dial on the safe. Mrs. Jenkins ducked under my arm and jumped onto a metal box on the floor. I let go of the dial.

Not my box. I hadn't seen it before. It was small like a money box. The latch on the front didn't have a lock.

I thumbed the latch and lifted the lid. Mrs. Jenkins looked in. No mouse. Instead there was a rectangular electronic device.

Brick looked over my shoulder. "SSD hard drive."

I grabbed a t-shirt and wiped my prints from the box. I wiped where Mrs. Jenkins had sat on it. Then I used the shirt to lift the box out of the closet.

I spun the tumblers on the gun safe, threw it open, and grabbed the Smith & Wesson M&P40. With the other hand I lifted the holster from its hook on the closet wall. Brick was holding the metal box, my shirt wrapped around it to keep his prints off.

My phone rang as we ran out to the Shelby. I fumbled the phone trying to answer. I could hear J'Leah's voice. I piled into the car. "Talk to me."

"Cali's not with Drummond. He's alone."

Both a real and a metaphorical whoosh left me.

Brick had the box in the back seat of the Shelby and jumped into the front.

"She's—"

"I heard." The Shelby fired up and Brick got us moving. He took the path we'd seen the Ghibli go. "Where to?"

I put the phone on speaker. "Where are you?"

J'Leah said, "You can follow with the app."

"I will. Where are you?"

"You're not going to believe this." She sounded calm, relaxed. "He stopped for gas."

Lucky again. That Ghibli must drink gas. I swiped to the tracker app. "We're in motion. Any idea where he's headed?"

"No idea. We're not near anything. Middle of nowhere.'"

"Airport?"

"Doesn't look like it."

"CDE?"

"No."

"To meet someone?"

"Could be?"

"Which direction is he headed then? Your best guess."

She took a second. "Indiana?"

The rain had started up again. A drizzle or a mist. Enough to wet the road. There was no one but us and the corn and soy fields. Brick pushed the Shelby faster.

J'Leah said, "Hang on. He's going into the store. If you hurry…"

We weren't going to make it. "Can you slow him down?"

"How physical do you want me to get?"

"Just block him in at the pumps or something. Get in front of him at the register."

"I can do that." The call ended.

Dusk was an hour away, but the clouds coming in turned everything prematurely gray. The Shelby hung tight to the road and we closed on Drummond.

My phone dinged. Text from J'Leah. Photo of her standing at a register next to displays of candy bars and peanuts. She was fingering a stick of beef jerky. Drummond was in the shot behind her.

I sent her a thumb and explained it to Brick.

A couple of minutes later another photo arrived. Blurry and streaked with raindrops. The Bolt blocking the Ghibli at the pumps. I explained it to Brick.

Brick kept his eyes on the road. "She's playing with him."

My phone rang. J'Leah. "Jig will be up in a minute unless you want me to get more aggressive."

Then the gas station appeared ahead of us. "Look to your left."

We could see the Bolt, and the Ghibli maneuvering around it.

J'Leah said, "Got you. What do you want me to do now?"

"Let him out. Let's see if we can get him to a less populated area."

"Roger that."

Brick and I passed J'Leah and kept the call open.

Drummond obliged my wish, like he was doing us a favor. Headed northwest on a rural road into nowhere. Like he really was driving to Indiana.

We hung back. Ghibli, Shelby, Bolt. A little parade. But Drummond didn't know he was part of the procession.

The road was empty. A few houses sat back from the berm. Some stretches of just fields. There was no reason for Drummond to recognize the Shelby, and he should only know the Bolt from the gas station. I spoke to Brick and into the phone. "Good a place as any."

Brick palmed the wheel. "I really don't want to scratch this car."

"Already did."

He winced and accelerated. "Plan?"

"Stop him. Get in front. J'Leah—"

"Got it. I'll close behind."

The Shelby made it easy. Sliced through rain and mist into the on-coming lane, cut a clean line around the Ghibli, and sliced back in front of Drummond.

Brick softened his foot on the accelerator. We slowed, Drummond slowed. The Bolt came up behind the Ghibli. The parade closed ranks.

Brick slowed more and drifted toward the center of the road. There was no way for Drummond to get around.

The Bolt drifted over toward the center of the road. We had him.

Then Drummond got skittish. The Ghibli lurched into the passing lane. The berm was steeply banked down into the fields. There wasn't room to pass.

Then the Ghibli's tires dropped off the far side of the road and the car swerved and skidded. Brick jerked the Shelby away and let the Ghibli through.

I stared at him.

"I said I don't want to scratch the paint again."

J'Leah's voice came over the phone. "What was that?"

Then the Ghibli braked hard in front of us and Brick had to slow fast. The Ghibli skidded into the entry of a long gravel drive and spun around. Rocks kicked up and the car fishtailed back onto the road and passed us going the opposite direction.

J'Leah was already turning around. Brick embarked on a three-point turn. "You had enough?"

"Just stop him. I'll pay for the paint."

J'Leah was in front of us. The little Bolt accelerated to the Ghibli's bumper. Brick shifted down and opened up the carburetors and took the Shelby into the other lane. Here we go again.

We came apace of the Ghibli. Drummond looked over. I looked over. The game was up. I pointed to the side of the road and mouthed *stop*.

He didn't. The Ghibli braked hard. J'Leah braked hard behind him. The Ghibli skidded. The Bolt was compact and heavy and hugged the road.

Then the back of the Ghibli kissed the Bolt. J'Leah kept the Bolt steady, but Drummond overcorrected and spun away. The Ghibli turned in a slow arc on the wet road, slipped off the berm, and punched a hole through a line of honeysuckle and trees and disappeared.

There was a thump, then nothing.

The shoulder had a flat, grassy area, and we pulled off the road just down from where the Ghibli left tracks through the mud. J'Leah was ahead and we could see her twisted around and reaching into the back seat of the Bolt.

I stepped out into the rain and walked up to J'Leah. She put her window down some. "Better hope he's OK."

I didn't disagree. J'Leah tugged herself into black rain gear and came out of the car.

Brick was walking toward the tracks to peer in at the hole in the brush where the Ghibli had gone through. A thin high-pitched whine rose from beyond the trees. Tires spinning.

My jacket wasn't waterproof. Rain seeped through. J'Leah and I joined Brick and we all took a closer look. The Ghibli wasn't visible. A jagged scar at bumper height on a middling walnut tree indicated what had probably caused the thump. The whining continued.

J'Leah put a hand up. "Let me go in and look." In the rain and gathering darkness, and with her black rain gear and dark skin, she was already almost a shadow.

She disappeared into the gap in the trees and greenery.

The whine of tires spinning was joined by the groan of the Ghibli engine racing. Brick and I waited and got wetter.

A minute or two later, J'Leah came back. "He seems OK. Well enough to try to get the car out of there, but he's stuck."

I looked at the others. "What do you think? Just call it in and let the locals sort it out?"

Brick wiped rainwater from his chin. "We've come this far. Let's play it out."

"You have a plan?"

He shrugged.

"There's no stairs out here to hang him over."

Brick turned toward the sounds of the tires and the engine. "Let's just go drag him out."

We didn't have to. The Ghibli's engine stopped and there was the sound of a car door thumping, then thumping again and again. Drummond screamed at the car, then we saw him slipping in the mud and tracks that punched through the tree line.

I grabbed Brick and J'Leah and spun. "Go."

They did. We retreated to the cars.

Drummond never saw us. We were fifty yards away in the rain and gray. We'd have been in clear enough view if he had looked. But he didn't. He gained purchase at the road, then he turned and walked away from us.

Brick reached for the Shelby door. "Let's go get him."

I put up a hand. "Wait a minute." I looked in the back of the Shelby at the floorboards where the metal box sat, still wrapped in my shirt.

J'Leah came over and looked in around me. "What is that?"

Brick had caught on. "Hard drive. Belongs to Drummond. But for some reason he wanted to leave it at Jackson's house."

J'Leah tipped her head up. "Explain."

Brick did, very quickly. Then he said, "We could give it back to Drummond."

I nodded. "That's what I was thinking."

J'Leah considered it. "You'd never know what's on it."

Rain pattered on J'Leah's gear. She looked dry. Brick and I were soaked.

J'Leah spoke first. "It could help wrap things up."

"Could." I pointed to Brick.

He looked down the road where Drummond had disappeared. No other cars had passed us since the Ghibli went off the road, no house lights had come on, and no one had approached. He opened the Shelby door. "Now's our chance."

J'Leah opted to let me and Brick do it. She stripped off her rain gear and jammed it into the Bolt, and she drove off.

Brick and I slogged through the rain and mud into the tracks left by the Ghibli. We pushed through the gash in the wet branches. The Ghibli was embedded in mud about twenty feet beyond, neatly sandwiched around undergrowth and saplings. The car was banged up. A rear fender hugged a skinny box elder. Mud was everywhere. The driver's door was dented and hung open. The trunk was damaged and popped open, and rain dripped in.

Brick carried the box to the car and walked around to the trunk. He dropped the box inside, pushed it out of the rain, and withdrew the shirt it had been wrapped in.

I slipped through the mud and reached under the car to remove the tracker. This time for good.

Then we dragged our feet through the footprints in the mud around Drummond's car. The rain was already starting to wash the prints away, but we dragged our steps through them anyway. An ounce of prevention is worth everything your grandmother told you it was.

We started back for the road. The Ghibli had a long gash down one side. One front tire had bent under the car. Drummond was never going to be able to drive it out. I said, "Waste of a good car."

Brick shrugged. "Eh."

22

I NEEDED TO CALL BRONIGAN. There was some rush, but Brick didn't want to get the car dirty. We stood in the rain and pulled off our muddy shoes. We tossed those in the trunk and added our wet socks and jackets. Then Brick grabbed the dog seat cover from the back and tried to drape that over the bucket seats in front. It was the best we could do.

Brick got the heater going and we pulled out and I called Bronigan. He answered on the second ring and said, "I was just thinking about you."

"I'll bet."

"You never called back about that thing at CDE."

"I'm doing that now. Actually, I could use a favor. It's timely."

"Uh-huh."

"I need the county sheriff out here to pick up a guy, and his car."

"I can arrange that."

"It's in Clark County."

"Then just call their non-emergency number. I can get that for you."

"I don't want a record of a call from my phone number."

Bronigan said, "Hold on." There was the sound of footsteps, then, "What's going on?"

"This particular vehicle and its driver are currently of interest with the FBI. The car is wrecked. The driver is walking away. The FBI are going to want both."

Bronigan said, "Talk to me."

"Can you check your bulletins?"

"I can." There was typing. Bronigan's radio squealed and he turned it down. Then he said one word: "DeLuna?"

"Bingo."

"Give me the exact location."

I did. "DeLuna was walking north along the road about ten minutes ago."

Bronigan said, "I'm going to have to jump on this. I'll be creative. You can tell me what it's about later."

"Promise. And Roger?"

"Yeah."

"Thanks."

He disconnected.

One down.

I stuck my feet to the blower to warm and dry them.

Brick turned the heat to the floor vents. "Well?"

"Bronigan's going to put them on it."

"Why didn't you just call the FBI guy?"

"I thought about it. It's messy. Wondering how much of us I can keep out of it."

Brick grunted. "We'll see."

I turned my feet under the warm air and called Cali. It went to message. I called Marzi. She answered and said, "Now will you tell me what's going on?"

"Where are you?"

"Tom's."

"Where's Cali?"

"She's here. With me."

"Why isn't she answering her phone or texts?"

A few seconds passed. "I don't think she wants to talk to you."

"Well she's going to. Put her on."

Cali's voice came through. It was flat. "Dad."

"You're OK?"

"Yes, I'm OK. Why are you asking that?"

"Why wouldn't you answer? Why wouldn't you talk to me?"

There was a moment of quiet. Too long for my liking. Then, "You weren't acting right."

Ouch. Double ouch.

Brick fiddled with the knobs on the dash and pretended not to hear.

I pressed the phone closer to my ear. "You're right."

Utter quiet.

"Cali?"

"Yeah?"

"You are the most important thing to me. If we have to make some changes, we can talk about that."

Another moment of quiet. "What does that mean?"

"If I have to look for a different kind of work, I can do that." I hadn't realized it until just then. But I knew I would follow through.

More quiet. "Why would you do that?"

"It's a long story, honey. Can we talk about it when I get home?"

"OK." A sniffle? "I know mom worried that something bad would happen to you. But it didn't. It happened to her."

My eyes misted a little.

Cali said, "I just don't want to be scared."

I misted some more.

She said, "That's why I didn't answer. Because I didn't want to be scared."

"I don't want you to be scared either."

"But it doesn't matter. I wasn't scared for mom, and she died. And I am scared for you, and you didn't. It doesn't matter."

But it did matter. "We'll talk about that later. Can you put Marzi back on now?"

Marzi came back on the line and said, "Are you going to tell me what this is all about?"

"Can I do that once, with the both of you?"

Marzi breathed. "I think that's for the best."

"I'm on my way. It'll all be over soon. Everything is going to be okay."

I almost believed it.

23

KAUFMAN CALLED in the morning. It was Sunday and I'd slept late. It was almost six-thirty.

The night before hadn't been what I expected. Once Cali and Marzi heard the story, their worries bothered them more than what had actually happened. I told them I would think about looking for another line of work if that's what it took to make everyone happy.

They thought about it over dinner. Then after we'd eaten and cleaned up, Cali and Marzi talked just the two of them in the kitchen while I sat out on the front porch in a sweatshirt.

The moon was big and bright and low and hung over the village like it was trying to give us all a big hug. I didn't mind so much being left outside. Mrs. Jenkins came out and prowled around my feet and got her head scratched, then she heard or sensed or imagined she heard or sensed something somewhere out in the village wilds, and she slinked off into the dark.

Cali and Marzi left me out there for a long time. I was getting tired and trying not to nod off. I had my feet up and they got cold and that helped me stay awake.

Then Cali came and got me and I went back inside and she and Marzi sat me on the couch in the living room. They faced me and said they thought they'd come to an important decision, but there was a question they needed to ask before they could be sure.

I was already thinking about what would come next. Maybe go back and finish college. I was good with numbers, maybe get into accounting or work toward a CPA. Maybe open a little business, home repair or light remodeling. A little painting and plumbing. Maybe try to flip houses or get a real estate license and sell them. None of it sounded great, but there was one thing I knew for sure: there was no way I could be a mall cop.

Just when all of that was spinning through my head, Cali asked me if all of us would be happy if I quit being a P.I. She meant me. Would I be happy.

I tried to get an answer out, but the words got stuck. That led to a long discussion about middle ground and making careful decisions and some other stuff. I admit I was too tired to follow all of it, but the gist was that maybe I would still be a P.I.

But now in the morning, that might depend on what happened with Kaufman. I shushed Mrs. Jenkins from my lap and turned my attention to Kaufman's call and my current situation.

Kaufman cleared his throat. "Jackson, sorry to wake you."

"You didn't wake me."

"Ah, you keep Bureau hours."

"If you say so."

"I say we need to talk."

"I've been expecting it." It sounded harsher than I'd meant, so I embellished. "It's Sunday. I assume you'd like to be with your family. Can we get this over with sooner rather than later?"

"I'd like that."

"You know where my office is."

It took him a moment to think about it. "That's sufficient. This needn't be in the Bureau office."

"I'll put on the coffee."

I picked up my jacket and went out to the truck.

There isn't much open in Yellow Springs at that hour on a Sunday. The businesses are locked up, and the restaurants haven't even begun to warm their grills yet. Even the churches are still asleep.

But not Dino's Cappuccinos. I stopped there and bought pastries and went up to my office.

The sky was just turning orange in the east when Kaufman arrived.

His shiny black shoes made an appearance as he maneuvered around the door, and then Kaufman appeared.

I looked past him into the hallway. "No Mister Anderson?"

Kaufman unfolded a chair and sat. "No Mister Anderson, but I did enjoy your joke."

Funny, he hadn't seemed to.

He had the shiny shoes, but Kaufman wasn't wearing the suit. I guess even the feds get a day to dress down. For Kaufman that meant khakis and a blue-and-white checked shirt. Black insulated windbreaker against the chill. I couldn't see the back of the jacket. Maybe FBI was printed there in big letters. If Kaufman was on his way to church, he didn't dress as nice for it as he did for his day job.

I was working my way through a scone. I poured coffee for Kaufman and waved a hand over other pastries on the desk.

Without a word, Kaufman picked up a sweet roll. We skipped the other preliminaries. Kaufman jumped in. "Why don't you run through it again for me?"

I expected this. I'd told it before, but I knew the procedure. Kaufman's notepad was out. He would be checking what I said for consistency against his notes.

I went through the whole thing again. Drummond hiring me, posed as Carlos. My break-in at CDE. Discovering that it was really Drummond. Brick and I confronting Drummond in his office and Drummond admitting that the project was faked and he set me up for cover. I added commentary about how inept that plan was.

I glossed over Brick hanging Drummond by his ankles. I skipped J'Leah entirely, including her breaching the CDE cyber systems and copying files. I left out the tracker and the car chase. I pretended not to know what I didn't say. I was deliberate and slow and tried to cover any stumbles over my words with attention to little bits of the scone I was eating. I played the dupe. Just a regular P.I. who stumbled onto a job that was a little bigger than he expected. Not smart enough to see his way out of it.

If Kaufman wasn't buying it, he put on a good pretense that he was. Maybe that was how they did it. Show some interest and nod a little, let the suspect spill what he shouldn't.

Kaufman said very little while I talked. He stopped occasionally to clarify a time or date or other little detail, but he mostly let me run with it. He flipped pages in his notepad, made some notes or marks, and tried to keep his sticky fingerprints off the paper as he worked and ate the sweet roll.

I finished my story and leaned back. "The whole thing seems pretty inane to me."

Kaufman tapped his notepad on his leg. "It's a head-scratcher. Bad plan from the start. The brothers had money, lots of it. Drummond was greedy…" He stopped himself as if he realized he was saying too much.

I pushed a napkin across the desk to him. "I'm interested."

Kaufman considered it for a moment, then let out a little more line. "Drummond took advantage of his brother being away in Mexico. He knew the money would slow down when it was discovered that the project hadn't gone anywhere, and it wasn't going to. Drummond wanted to keep the government money flowing. But the government wasn't getting anything for its money, and he wanted to hide that."

"Why pretend the material had been stolen? Is that even plausible?"

Kaufman went quiet. I figured that was it. End of story. Classified FBI business. But then he picked up the thread again. "It's not plausible, as you say. Drummond was the glad-hander. The salesman. A guy who was used to being able to persuade anybody of anything. He appeared to think he could just brass it through."

I waited. Kaufman didn't say more, so I fished. "You've got to be kidding me."

Kaufman shook his head.

"So Drummond isn't exactly the smart one."

"It doesn't seem so."

It still didn't really make sense. "What about Carlos? Did he know any of it?"

"Carlos DeLuna has been with his wife in Mexico City, where she is undergoing treatment for cancer. This you know. The Bureau has been in contact with Carlos. A couple of our agents are down there to depose him. My personal feelings…" He leaned away, as if he was having second thoughts about revealing anything personal. But he leaned back and went on. "I don't think Carlos knew anything about what Drummond had planned, or what he was doing. Carlos knew the project was a bust, and he was planning on spinning down CDE Enterprises once the final report came out. He was ready to sell."

So that much had been true. One of the brothers wanted to sell. "Carlos' wife is really named Judy?"

"Affirmative. Carlos and Judy have been married since they met in college in at Universidad Nacional Autónoma de México."

So that was true too. "So Drummond just assumed Carlo's role—house, job, office, even his wife's name."

"That's a fair account."

I wanted to know about the black box. The hard drive inside it. The smashed-up Ghibli and apprehending Drummond. But I wasn't supposed to know any of that. And I didn't want Kaufman to ask about the cyber check or anything that might sniff out a trail to J'Leah. I switched gears to keep the conversation going while I worked out how to keep fishing and avoid the potholes. "Do you have any news on how Judy is doing?"

It might have seemed a strange thing to ask. I had never met Carlos or Judy. I knew them only as stories told by Drummond. But somehow I felt a connection to Carlos and his wife.

Kaufman may have shared the feeling. He brightened. "Judy is doing better. The cancer may be in remission."

Fingers of sunlight tittered at the window. I eyed another pastry. And I went back to something that had really been bothering me. "Why would Drummond pose as Carlos at all? Why not just hire me as himself? He's one of the principles in the company."

"Why do any of it? Carlos and Drummond could have just cashed out. Sold the business. Done nothing—shut down and retired with their piles of money. They didn't need the failed project. If one or both of them wanted to go on, they could have simply looked for other work, as they've been successful doing."

"The failed project wouldn't have put them out of business?"

"Not by a long shot."

"It would have hurt their business? Lowered the value of CDE?"

Kaufman shrugged. "I don't suppose you know much about government contracts? CDE was lucrative. It would have continued to be. Projects fail all the time."

"Then why would Drummond…"

"He was greedy."

Kaufman and I looked at each other. I considered us. Two working men, sitting in a tiny little office very early on a Sunday morning, trying to make sense of why other men did what they did. I sighed. "There's an art to being happy with what you've got."

Kaufman agreed. He leaned to me like he was telling a secret. "And that's a lot easier to do when you have multiple millions. Drummond has no excuse. Who couldn't be happy with what he had?"

Indeed.

Kaufman tucked his notepad away.

I took in the glow of light rising in the window. It looked like we were wrapping up. I turned to Kaufman. "Am I likely to be deposed?"

"Possible." He tipped his head. "Maybe even likely. The best way to try to avoid that would be for you to give your consent to a search. We would look at your office, your home, and your electronic devices. I don't want to have to do that to you, but I think it's the best way to try to avoid the Bureau pursuing a warrant. And it may clear you out of the investigation most efficiently."

It felt too easy. I didn't know if Kaufman was having a heartfelt moment, if there was more to come, or if he was playing me. Maybe all of those. It didn't matter. I wasn't the one dealing the cards. I would take what I could get. "And what about my daughter's things?"

"I don't think we have cause to want to look at her possessions. Right now. But I won't get to make that decision. I can make a recommendation."

I believed him. But my track record recently wasn't great. I'd just been fooled by a fool. Drummond DeLuna had duped me, and I bought it.

There were still some elephants in the room. I didn't want to point them out if Kaufman couldn't see them—or didn't feel the need to bring them up. I eyed the pastries again. "Is that all?"

"That's all that I can presume at this point."

I didn't know what that meant. FBI talk, or lawyer talk. But he hadn't mentioned J'Leah. That was good, and I wanted to keep it that way. I tapped some fingers on the desk. "Sounds agreeable so far."

Then Kaufman stiffened. "Before we go further, there is one more thing."

An elephant.

"We have Drummond, uh…in the Bureau's confines."

I didn't ask what that meant. I hoped I'd never have to find out.

"It was a little unusual how we found him. It appears that Drummond was headed—" he took out his notepad again, looked for something, then tucked the pad away again—"for the Indianapolis airport."

I felt a smile coming. I tried to stop it.

Kaufman noticed.

I suppressed the smile. But I was going to tell J'Leah she was right that Drummond was headed to Indiana.

Kaufman continued. "Drummond planned to fly to Mexico City to try to convince his brother to keep going with the ruse he'd created."

I nodded like it meant something to me.

"But here's the unusual thing. Drummond was on foot when we found him."

Kaufman looked like he expected a reaction, and I hadn't given him one. I tried one out. "On foot?"

"Walking."

I kept my expression flat.

"In the rain."

I blinked. "Long walk to Indianapolis?"

Kaufman tapped his knee. "There is something I have to ask you, and it may change what we've talked about."

"Mmm?"

"Drummond's car went off the road. He says he saw something when that happened."

I waited. So did Kaufman. He looked like he could wait all day. Finally, I said, "Something?"

"A sports car. An old one."

"Hmm."

"Drummond says it looked like you were riding in the passenger seat of that car."

I searched for the right reaction. Surprise? Shock? Denial? I went with confusion. "Huh?"

"It's not clear how Drummond went off the road. He seems to think someone was following him, but the details he describes aren't coherent or consistent."

Kaufman let a long moment pass. I resisted the urge to fill it this time.

When I didn't offer anything, Kaufman picked up again. "Drummond was distressed. He'd taken…something non-prescription to relax him. His recollections of those events have so far been…not reasonable or reliable."

That meant not admissible. That was good.

Another long moment passed. Kaufman hadn't asked a question yet. Maybe he wouldn't. Then he said, "Your friend Darnell Brickman owns a vintage car. A sports car." He paused. "A black and gold 1966 Shelby GT-350." He said it without looking at his notes.

I didn't need to say anything. There was no question here. I offered up, "He does."

We both knew the game. Again, Kaufman sat for a long time without asking his question. I took the opportunity to fill the void in my own way. "Brick sure loves that old car."

Kaufman tapped his knee some more. "Do you have any further comment on the…matter?"

I nodded agreeably. "Cool car. Brick's Shelby. He sure loves it. But it's not exactly my thing, you know? Nothing beats an old pickup."

Kaufman grinned. I could tell he hadn't planned to. "It's quite a co-incidence, Drummond thinking he saw a blue sports car and your friend driving that particular vehicle."

There's a reason P.I.s don't like coincidences. This wasn't a coinci-dence. But I needed to keep making it look like one. I reached for a pastry as a distraction. "I guess it was on his mind."

Kaufman played dumb. "Hmm?"

I took a bite and chewed. "Guy drove a Ghibli. He knew something about cars."

Kaufman adjusted himself on the little folding chair. If he'd been wearing a tie, this is where he would reach up and straighten it. "You don't see a reason why Drummond would think he saw you when his car went off the road?"

I licked a shred of pastry from a finger. "Maybe he saw the Shelby when Brick and I went to his office. It was Drummond's kind of thing. Brick gets all kinds of comments on that car."

Kaufman frowned.

"Like I said, I guess it was on Drummond's mind."

Kaufman didn't look all the way convinced.

I added, "You said Drummond had, uh, partaken of something. Seems like his brain was a little scrambled."

Kaufman sat stiffly like he had a board up his back.

I gave him time to simmer on it. I'd had plenty of pastry, but I kept eating to show it didn't mean anything to me. Just musing. Whatever.

Eventually Kaufman softened and closed his notepad. "I guess there's no way to know."

I shrugged. Who cares? I have a pastry to eat.

Kaufman pulled his jacket tighter but he didn't get up. "Is there anything else you'd like to ask me?"

There were several things. But I kept my mouth shut about them. Let the elephants have the room.

Then I did ask one thing. I smiled and said, "How are your kids on this fine Sunday morning?"

He grinned. "Still sleeping."

I smiled more. Gestured to the pastries still sitting on my desk. "Why don't you take these home for them?"

"No, I couldn't."

I held the smile. "It would make me happy."

Kaufman must have seen something in it. He softened. "You sure you wouldn't mind?"

I didn't. Dino's was just downstairs. I'd stop and pick up more to take home for Cali. And Dino's would still be the only thing open when I got back down to the street.

Kaufman folded the pastries into a napkin I offered and tucked that into his jacket pocket. Then we rose and we shook hands, like good people do.

Kaufman left, and I closed up my little office and walked down into the sunlight. The sky was full orange in the east. The clouds had gone. I thought for sure things were clearing up now. They just had to be.

24

A COUPLE OF THINGS happened quickly. Brick and I spent much of that first day after Kaufman's visit memorizing and re-memorizing our stories over the heavy bag and some serious lifting of the heaviest objects. We compared details, who knew what, who didn't know what, who knew what when, and what to leave out. It was carefully crafted and we went over it again and again and tried to anticipate what we weren't thinking of that we might be asked.

Call it revisionist if you want, but this was the FBI. We wanted to be prepared. My brain was frazzled by the time we were done, and so were my muscles. At least no one got hung over the edge of the hayloft by their ankles.

J'Leah made the files she'd copied from CDE and all traces of them disappear. I didn't know details, and I didn't want to know. That was her job. They were just gone. No one knew that J'Leah had breached CDE cyber security or copied files, not even Drummond. We intended to keep it that way.

I prepared a report as Kaufman had asked, indicating that the Jackson Flint Detective Agency had been hired to perform both physical and cyber security checks of CDE. Details related to the physical check matched the report and events as recorded by the Clark County sheriff's office when they responded to the call on the night I entered the compound beneath the fence line. Bronigan helped with some details there. Details in my report to Kaufman matched exactly details Brick and I had memorized.

I took Bronigan to lunch and told him what I could. It wasn't as much as he wanted to know, and there wasn't anything in it that looked like it was going to help him. Bronigan didn't mind. He was up for a promotion to day shift, and that would get him home with his wife and little boy at more reasonable hours. We celebrated over slices of pie for dessert, and I bought a whole one for him to take home.

The FBI skipped further interviews and went straight to depositions from me and Brick. We didn't take it as a good sign. A deposition meant somebody thought there might be a trial or further testimony. But Kaufman insisted this would give the agency leverage that might preclude our further involvement. It was more lawyer talk, but Brick and I were deposed. We didn't have a choice.

Brick's deposition was interesting because one of the lawyers in the room had seemed as interested in the GT-350 as he was in asking Brick questions about Drummond DeLuna. Brick had showed the guy pictures and videos and they chatted and he did everything except invite the guy to see the Shelby and take a ride in it. I guess FBI lawyers are real people too.

There was no warrant, but I agreed to a search. It was perfunctory. Agents looked around my office and the house, took my laptop and phone for a day, and returned everything. They let Cali alone.

After that, things went back to normal with work, which meant boring things. I was fine with that. I got contacted with a job offer from a client I'd worked with before. It was tracking down bail jumpers and serving paper. I didn't really care for the work, but it was straightforward and familiar, and I was good at it. Easy money.

That work was also relatively safe, and there was no FBI. That helped on the home front. I was leaving for my work after Cali went to school, getting home before she did, and planning meals and home life around her. And around Marzi.

It turned out that neither Cali nor Marzi had the will to ask me to quit being a P.I. Once I'd made the offer, that took much of the energy out of it. Cali was reminded that I'd quit the Sheriff's in part as a concession to her mother. The three of us bumped along on that front, keeping the boat in the water but not quite knowing for sure that all of the holes had been patched.

It helped that I was home and my work was so quiet it was invisible to them. It also helped that the Smith & Wesson stayed locked in the gun safe in the closet.

I never met Carlos DeLuna or his wife Judy, but I wondered how they were doing. I had a feeling I would have liked the guy.

A couple of weeks went by, and the FBI seemed to have lost interest in me and Brick. J'Leah stayed entirely off their radar. I paid to have the fender on the Bolt repaired. Then both Brick and I got courtesy messages from Kaufman that he anticipated they wouldn't need anything more from us. They must have gotten their man.

The most surprising thing was that Brick just stopped mentioning Quando. I brought up the question while we were running up the devil's backbone and he dismissed it. Ran away to avoid talking about Quando and almost beat me to the top. I didn't bring it up again, and neither did Brick. It was like all traces of the kid had been wiped away. I think that's what Brick needed to move on.

Then about a week later, right when the frosts were starting to come regular at night and the leaves were either bright and colorful or brown and muted, my phone dinged. There was a text from Brick, and there was only one word. *Come.*

I did.

I parked in the empty yard where the ruins of the old Skylark lay in a ghostly shadow of the original car. Brick wasn't in sight. I zipped my jacket and stepped out. Brittle grass and weeds and leaves crunched as I walked toward the barn.

I stopped when the cabin door opened. Brick waved me in.

I tramped over, hoping this meant coffee. Usually it was just a work-out and water.

Brick held a hand up for quiet when I entered. He pointed through an archway that opened to the kitchen. Someone stood at the stove with a spatula in hand, watching a pan. I moved to get a better view. It was Quando.

I whispered. "What's he doing?"

"Making a grilled cheese sandwich."

Quando flipped the sandwich and watched the pan some more.

"Is that good?"

Brick's eyes were wide. "I think so."

I motioned to the door. Brick lifted a sweatshirt from a hook and we went out.

I closed the door behind us. "What happened?"

"He just showed up."

"Just showed up?"

Brick shrugged.

"When?"

"About an hour ago."

"An hour? How—What's he been doing?"

Brick paced toward the car parts. "Eating."

"Eating?"

"For like the whole hour." He sat on the rusted engine block.

I sat across from him on a piece of chassis.

Brick explained. "He just showed up. Door was unlocked, he just walked in. Didn't knock, nothing. Hasn't called or texted or answered a message that whole time he was gone, and then he just walks in."

"Without a word?"

"He said *hey*."

A redtail hawk circled above in a thermal, its wings glinting against the sun when they tipped in the rising air. Looking for something to hunt. The circle of life. "You talk to him?"

"A little."

"What'd he say?"

Brick adjusted himself on the cold metal. "Said he needed to know if he could live with his mom."

I didn't say anything for a time. What was there to say? When it came to me, I spoke. "He could have told you. What he was doing."

"Yeah."

Now Brick didn't speak for a time. Then he adjusted his seat on the engine block. "Maybe it's OK that he didn't let me know. If he hadn't come back…"

The hawk passed out of the thermal, glided down, and looked for a way back into the updraft. We both watched it.

Then I said, "Why can't he live with his mother?"

Brick kept looking at the hawk. "Don't know. Maybe some day he'll tell me."

"But not today?"

"No. Today he's eating."

A breeze drifted out of the trees. Leaves dropped and tumbled in the draft. Brick shifted again. "Before he left, Quando said he'd tell me when he knew."

The redtail drifted to a pine and alit on a high branch. "When he knew what?"

"If he should stay here."

A ruckus of crows sounded from somewhere. Half a dozen corvids appeared in the sky and launched themselves into the air against the redtail in the pine. Mobbing. The smaller birds were protecting themselves from the predator.

Brick took it all in. "I think that's why he left."

I looked at the cabin and the kitchen window where I could almost see Quando inside. "To see if he should stay?"

"Yeah."

It was an odd way of doing it. I turned my gaze from the birds to Brick. "Did he say? If he's decided?"

Brick's eyes came down. "I think coming back was his answer."

I guessed that sounded right. "Is that what you want? For him to stay?"

I already knew the answer. Brick said it as if he hadn't been sure until now, but I think he always knew. "I'm going to call S.T."

The lawyer.

He stood. "See if we can get it done."

The crows swooped and cawed. The redtail raised its wings and lifted from the pine. The crows bobbed and dodged and pestered the hawk. I watched. "Big responsibility."

"It is. If it's what Quando wants, we'll try to make it work."

Quando. Last Brick had mentioned him, Brick called Quando the kid. Now we were back to Quando. I didn't mention it.

The redtail high-tailed it out of there, the smaller birds chattering behind. The murder of crows had won. For now.

Brick squinted up at the sky. It was empty of flight now. Empty, but waiting for the next story to tell.

He walked toward the house. "I have a lot to do."

Then he went inside and left me sitting in the yard on the old Buick. He did have a lot to do.

My butt was cold, so I got up and drove home. A grilled cheese sandwich sounded good.

Later when I told Cali that Quando was back, it interested her more than I expected. Then that night she told me she'd been wanting to host a dinner party. But not with her friends, and not just with me and Marzi. She wanted Brick and Quando. She took his return as a sign.

I didn't think it was such a good idea, but Cali was persistent. Marzi and I fell in line quickly enough. To get Brick, she had to agree to have the dinner at his cabin.

That was weird. Brick didn't generally like people coming to his place. He didn't even really want folks to know where he lived. But Brick thought Quando might do better if we had the dinner out at his cabin.

I didn't exactly encourage it, but Cali kept plodding along. We agreed to the Saturday after Thanksgiving. Everyone would get their turkey on Thursday. Leftovers on Friday. Saturday would be Cali's. And she was going to get her bouillabaisse.

As it turned out, Cali wanted to host with a lot of help from me and Marzi. That was fine for everyone. The three of us spent that Saturday shopping for groceries, chopping, and prepping. Marzi learned what *mise en place* is.

The evening was cold but not freezing. When we arrived at Brick's with the food and fixings, there was a dog running in the yard. Angelita Rojas Flores came out to help us carry things in, and I made the connection. The dog was Angelita's.

Brick came out and put a cold Dortmunder lager into my hand. I twisted the top off and we clinked bottles and drank beer while the food got carried in.

It was cramped in the kitchen. Marzi was there with Cali setting up the big pot on the stove to cook the bouillabaisse. Angelita was carrying linens and plates and settings to the table in the little dining room. It was cramped there too.

Brick and I retreated to the little living room. Two chairs, an end table, a mantle over a stone fireplace. On the table was a vase of cut flowers. I pointed.

Brick sipped his beer. "Yeah, finally got them." Carnations. Red. Rojas Flores.

Marzi came out with a cutting board. On it were stacked a baguette, knife, olive oil, and a serving plate. "You boys make yourself useful with the crostini." She smiled at Brick. "That grill you have outside works?"

He set his beer on the cutting board with the other things and accepted the whole package. "Yes, ma'am."

We went out. We knew a kitchen pass when someone handed us one.

We set up at the stone grill. It was old, like something out of a state park. Maybe that's where it had come from.

Quando was across the yard in a sweatshirt. He had buds stuffed into his ears and he tossed a Frisbee to the dog, who was very excited to chase the disc.

Brick went to the barn and came back with paper and tinder for the grill. We laid that into the pit and lit it. When the tinder smoked and caught and began to pull a draft up the stone chimney, we fed in some larger fuel. Then we stood and watched the grill warm and drank more Dortmunder.

Quando was still listening to whatever played on his earbuds and occasionally tossing the Frisbee for the dog. I was wondering what the odds were we could get him to come over with us when Cali came outside bundled in her coat.

She passed by me and Brick and went straight to Quando. I tried not to show my surprise.

Cali and Quando talked. I knew that Brick had gotten Quando into the school. I guessed that was working out and Cali and Quando were getting to know each other.

I laid the baguette out on the board to slice it, but Brick set his beer down and walked away. He went straight toward Cali and Quando.

I set the knife down and followed.

Cali and Quando were talking and looking at their phones. Cali had earbuds in. The dog squatted in the grass and wiggled its back end, hankering for another run after the Frisbee.

Brick took hold of the Frisbee and lined up a toss.

Cali pulled the buds from her ears, and the music from them drifted quietly on the wind.

Quando listened. "What did you say this is?" He gave a very obvious side-eye to me and Brick.

The music from the earbuds grew louder. It was something I recognized. Something I'd heard Cali listening to. Wolf Alice. Blush. A song about searching for happiness.

Cali and Quando listened to the song together. Brick tossed the Frisbee again. It floated in a wide arc and slipped sideways into the weeds.

The dog dove into the bramble and searched for the disc. He scrambled in the wrong direction.

Brick went to point the dog the right way.

It was then that Quando turned. He held his hand out to me and something in it glinted.

It was a penny.

Quando extended his hand. The wheat penny. He hadn't thrown it into the woods. "Take it."

I watched Brick with the dog. I thought about Cali with Quando. Thought about Marzi and Angelita inside. This whole thing. "You sure?"

Quando shrugged. "I don't need a penny."

I picked it up. The copper was shiny in the sunlight. Like he'd polished it.

I held the penny up and examined it. Lincoln on the front and two shafts of wheat on the back. *E pluribus unum.* Out of many, one.

Quando watched me. "Happy now?"

I was. I tucked the penny away for safekeeping. I wanted to have it and remember that feeling the next time things got funky.

Gratitude

Thank you for reading. If there's anything you liked about this book, will you please consider leaving a review on Amazon? That helps promote the book, and it encourages writers like me.

You can also **follow me on Amazon** and/or **sign up for email notices** at scottgeisel.com. I won't send more than a few emails per year – only to announce new books or other big news.

Other Novels in the Jackson Flint Series

Fair Game

A rainy night on a back road. He knew it was a bad idea to stop. A mysterious teen and a woman missing more than twenty years. A family secret and the homeless underworld.

Water To Bind

An old cabin in the woods. Mysterious visitors. A troubled teen. Family secrets. Whispered stories of a lost treasure. A legacy that stretches back into America's dark past. What is the secret of the cabin?

Jackson Flint Short Stories

Masquerade
Escape Velocity

Other Novels

Miller Knew: An Appalachian Noir and Suspense Story

Deep in the Appalachian hills, a brother and sister are in trouble. Miller's ma is gone. His pa is gone. Now they've come for him. Miller knows the kind of men who inhabit these hills. He doesn't want to become one of them. How can he protect himself and his sister without losing his soul?

www.ingramcontent.com/pod-product-compliance
Lightning Source LLC
Chambersburg PA
CBHW060431180626
46817CB00007B/2764